G R JORDAN

None Too Precious

A Highlands and Islands Detective Thriller #44

First edition

ISBN (print): 978-1-917497-22-0
ISBN (digital): 978-1-917497-21-3

This book was professionally typeset on Reedsy.
Find out more at reedsy.com

Chess is all about getting the king into check, you see. It's about killing the father. I would say that chess has more to do with the art of murder than it does with the art of war.

Arturo Pérez-Reverte

Contents

Foreword

The events of this book, while based around real and also fictitious locations around the UK, are entirely fictional and all characters do not represent any living or deceased person. All companies are fictitious representations and locations have been modified for the purposes of the story. This novel is best read while wearing a large crown—but keep your head down!

Acknowledgments

To Ken, Jean, Colin, Evelyn, John and Rosemary for your work in bringing this novel to completion, your time and effort is deeply appreciated.

Books by G R Jordan

The Highlands and Islands Detective series (Crime)

1. Water's Edge
2. The Bothy
3. The Horror Weekend
4. The Small Ferry
5. Dead at Third Man
6. The Pirate Club
7. A Personal Agenda
8. A Just Punishment
9. The Numerous Deaths of Santa Claus
10. Our Gated Community
11. The Satchel
12. Culhwch Alpha
13. Fair Market Value
14. The Coach Bomber
15. The Culling at Singing Sands
16. Where Justice Fails
17. The Cortado Club
18. Cleared to Die
19. Man Overboard!
20. Antisocial Behaviour
21. Rogues' Gallery
22. The Death of Macleod - Inferno Book 1

Kirsten Stewart Thrillers (Thriller)

1. A Shot at Democracy
2. The Hunted Child
3. The Express Wishes of Mr MacIver
4. The Nationalist Express
5. The Hunt for 'Red Anna'
6. The Execution of Celebrity
7. The Man Everyone Wanted
8. Busman's Holiday
9. A Personal Favour
10. Infiltrator
11. Implosion
12. Traitor

Jac Moonshine Thrillers

1. Jac's Revenge
2. Jac for the People
3. Jac the Pariah

Siobhan Duffy Mysteries

1. A Giant Killing
2. Death of the Witch
3. The Bloodied Hands
4. A Hermit's Death

The Contessa Munroe Mysteries (Cozy Mystery)

1. Corpse Reviver
2. Frostbite
3. Cobra's Fang

The Patrick Smythe Series (Crime)

1. The Disappearance of Russell Hadleigh
2. The Graves of Calgary Bay
3. The Fairy Pools Gathering

Austerley & Kirkgordon Series (Fantasy)

1. Crescendo!
2. The Darkness at Dillingham
3. Dagon's Revenge
4. Ship of Doom

Supernatural and Elder Threat Assessment Agency (SETAA) Series (Fantasy)

1. Scarlett O'Meara: Beastmaster

Island Adventures Series (Cosy Fantasy Adventure)

1. Surface Tensions

Dark Wen Series (Horror Fantasy)

Chapter 01

L ife was tough, certainly as tough as Emma MacTavish had ever known it. Not that Tommy wasn't a blessing. Of course he was. The little lad in the pram was so precious when he just lay there, sleeping in her arms. He was so adorable when she picked him up and he gurgled at her. So delightful when he blew those little bubbles out of his mouth.

And he was absolute hell when he cried the house down throughout the night. Like last night. Was it colic? Wind? Was it nappy rash? And she checked everything. She would pick him up and tap his back. Jiggle him about. Feed him that stuff they recommended for him, to make the wind escape. Then, just as he'd got off to sleep, his bottom would explode, and the dirty nappy would set him off again.

It would help if she had somebody else there with her—a husband, a boyfriend, someone to take Tommy. Not his dad. He was never getting back into the house; he would never get to see Tommy.

She'd had enough of being slapped about, had enough of the abuse, and she'd had to be tough to throw him out, to tell him no. She also needed a bit of help to do that, obviously, and thankfully, she had some friends who were strong.

Emma stopped for a moment. She thought about some of

the men who had helped her. They were good friends, but they were also taken.

It looked like Tommy and she were going to be a pair. They would have to stay a pair. How many people wanted a woman with a baby, after all? Especially one that screamed the house down.

Emma had come out that morning into town, because Tommy was probably at his happiest when he was in the pram. Was it the wind that was trapped in him which shifted about and came out when the pram jostled along the street? She wasn't sure. And that was the thing, wasn't it?

Nobody was sure. Nobody could say it was this, it was that. How did we not know after all this time how babies worked?

Emma had no shopping to do. So, she had moseyed around, checking shop windows. She'd even gone into some stores to look at outfits. Not that she needed an outfit. Where was she going? You didn't have to dress nice to go down to the mum and baby group. They'd accept you however you were. That was nice. She felt supported. It was still hard, though.

Inverness city centre was its usual busy self. Shoppers running here and there, trying to avoid the occasional bit of rain that seemed to be about today. Other than that, it was becoming spring, and while not the sunbathing weather, it was certainly getting warmer. She felt it when she pushed the pram. In the winter, there was never any sweat on her, not unless she was heavily wrapped up. But now, the exertion brought out a thin sheen to her face.

Not that Emma was unfit. Yes, she wasn't as fit as she had been. She'd been a runner back in the day before Tommy, and she enjoyed it. She didn't run now. Running would require somebody to look after Tommy, and she couldn't do that. She'd tried and asked the gym if she could bring him in the pram, but they weren't up for it.

The gym membership had cost a lot of money back when she had just her. And it was worth it. But they'd gone very snooty at the idea of a mum bringing her baby in with her. It wasn't the right look for their gym, where everyone had to look pristine. Well, Emma didn't think she looked bad, but things had changed, and being pristine wasn't top of the agenda anymore.

Emma pushed the pram here and there for another ten minutes, and realised that Tommy had gone quiet. *This could be it*, she thought. She spied a small cafe in the covered market. She made her way inside. Carefully, she stopped the pram beside a table, let go with delicate hands, and tried not to say anything. The cafe wasn't that busy, and she was close to the door, which thankfully was shut behind her. A covered market always had its noises outside, and she wanted nothing to wake Tommy up. She tucked the blanket in and smiled at him.

He always had a little frown on his face, especially when he slept. She did not know why, but she watched the little chest rise and fall. Her boy was as content as he'd been within the last three hours, and certainly since last night. He'd probably want to feed soon. Well, that would be another trauma. Put the food into him, and the wind kicked off, and then the entire cycle began again. She was sure he eventually slept because he was simply exhausted.

Emma reached down into her pocket, found her purse, and quickly made her way over to the counter. She glanced back and then turned to look at the array of goodies that the cafe offered. She picked out a croissant, asked for a coffee, and then engaged in a little chat with the young girl behind the till.

The young girl turned away for a moment, disappeared into the back, before coming out with a fresh coffee cup.

She made the coffee, gave it along with the croissant to Emma on a small tray, and Emma returned back to the table. She sat down, poured the two sugars into the coffee—saying it was all right as she was still within those early stages of motherhood and couldn't be expected not to take on energy— before she plopped a bit of milk in and stirred the coffee.

Emma sat back in the seat, lifted the coffee to her lips, and sipped it. *Yes*, she thought, *this was better*. She looked over at some customers. There was a man with his back to her, dressed in a modern suit. He seemed to lift his coffee delicately, before placing it back down and made his way up to the counter. There were some other women there, nattering away over a coffee and a bun. There was a man working on his laptop. They all seemed friendly enough, but nobody came over to you and said hello when you had a baby.

Then again, probably best that they didn't disturb Tommy. The man in the smart suit turned at the counter and looked over at her, giving a smile. He had a rather strange cravat on, which made her think he was an actor, but he seemed to carry a rather serious air about him. He returned to the seat he'd come from, his back once again to her.

Emma relaxed and took this time to herself. She pulled out her mobile to scroll through some of the banal messages and adverts and then switched it off. *People didn't message much anymore, either. You just got out of circulation. That was it*, she thought. *Just out of circulation. Still, he's worth it. My little man is worth it.*

She put her hand on the pram and rocked it back and forward gently. He'd be waking up in a minute. He never slept for that long. It was tough getting him to stay asleep. For the next couple of minutes, she continued the rocking, looking around her and sipping on her coffee. There was no sound from the pram. That was bliss.

Emma wondered, could she get another coffee? Could she keep Tommy asleep? If she went up and ordered another one, would it be a waste of money because he would wake up? Maybe she should get a takeaway. She decided that was for the best, approached the counter, ordered and came back, placing her paper cup on the table. Tommy was awfully quiet.

Emma leaned over and looked inside the pram. The blanket was pulled back. Tommy wasn't there.

Her stomach went like a knot, tightening and tightening and tightening. Her eyes went wide, looking around. She could feel her legs wobble.

'Tommy,' she said, barely audible as the breath was stolen from her with the panic ripping through her. 'Tommy, where's Tommy? Tommy!' Suddenly, she inhaled deeply and let out a roar. 'Tommy!' she cried. 'Where's Tommy?' The surrounding people looked over, faces bemused. 'My baby!' she shouted. 'Where's my baby?'

The man in the rather smart suit leapt from his chair and turned to her. 'Excuse me, ma'am. Are you missing your child?'

'Tommy,' she said. 'He was there! Tommy was there!' She pointed into the pram.

'You had a child with you? You came in with a child in that pram?' said the man.

'Yes! My child was with me! He's gone! I was just in here and he's gone! Where is he? Where the hell is he? What?'

'Stay calm,' said the man, and reached inside his jacket. 'My name's Detective Constable Eric Patterson. We'll get a search party for your child. Stay calm.'

Patterson turned and pointed to a woman. 'You, ma'am. Get her a glass of water and get her sitting down.' Patterson picked up his phone and dialled the station.

'DC Patterson. I'm in the city's covered marketplace, in the coffeehouse. We have a child potentially taken. I need assistance now. Everything you can get, converge on my location. I'm getting people to come, okay?' Patterson said to the woman. 'What's your name?'

'Emma,' said the woman.

'Surname?'

'MacTavish,' she said. 'He's gone. Tommy. Tommy's gone.'

'What's Tommy wearing?'

'Blue jeans. He's got a green jumper on. He's not got much hair.'

'What size is he? How old?' asked Patterson.

'Six months.'

Patterson could feel his own stomach tighten. He turned to the people around. 'Anyone see someone come in? Come in quickly and go?'

Everyone shook their head.

'Nobody leaves here, okay? Everyone stays. Get Emma to drink some water,' he said to the woman beside her. Patterson stepped outside of the coffeehouse. He looked around, left and right, trying to spot anyone with a child. He saw a woman carrying a child and ran over towards her.

'Excuse me, ma'am. DC Eric Patterson. Can I ask, is that your child?'

The woman looked at him as if he was insane. 'Of course, it's my child,' she said.

'I know this is going to sound weird, but we've just had a

child lifted. Can I ask that you stand over by that coffeehouse for me for a minute, please?' He produced his warrant card, showing it to her. 'I'm totally serious,' he said.

She walked over, and he saw another child in a pram. *No, that child was two or three years of age. That was no good.* He looked up and heard footsteps running in towards the coffeehouse. He put his hand up, spying a couple of police constables.

'DC Patterson here,' he said. 'Child's been lifted within the last ten minutes. Close off the shopping centre. Close off the marketplace. Nobody in, nobody out. Then search for someone with a child. See if there's anyone in here. Then we get a bigger picture.'

Patterson swept a hand through his hair. He could feel the sweat on his own brow. This was a six-month-old. This was a kid. The two constables with him turned and ran off towards the exits. More were arriving now, and he'd need to operate from a central point.

He couldn't charge off himself, and so he started pulling some officers towards him. He organised a central point where he would stay with Emma. Uniform closed down the marketplace. They brought every child that was still within it to the coffeehouse. Meanwhile, officers were driving around the streets looking for babies, stopping and interviewing parents.

Emma was in shock. She was shaking, and Patterson had to get paramedics to her. He'd got a description out of her—brief, simple—but she would not be much more use now. *Did she have a partner who could come and take her? What was her home life?* That could wait. The search was key. The police search coordinator would come soon. Patterson would hand over everything, but until then, he'd keep everyone on the move. He'd grab a radio off one of his uniformed colleagues, checking in with the searchers. Nothing was forthcoming. Little Tommy wasn't anywhere.

Two hours later, Patterson left the scene. No child had been found. He'd been in the coffeehouse himself. He'd had his back to the door. And now he sat down and tried to write what had happened. What had he heard? Had there been voices? But there'd been nothing. He'd seen Emma come up to the counter and go back. The child—had there even been one in the pram? He'd never heard a noise out of it. He hadn't looked. As he made his way back to the station and up the stairs towards his office within the arts section, Patterson could feel himself shake.

They hadn't got Tommy. There was guilt pouring over him. Patterson had been on the scene. He should have done something. But he hadn't even known the child was missing. He hadn't even really known if there'd been a child. He'd just sat with his coffee. So, he wandered into the office and sat down at his desk. There was paperwork to do. He'd have to get on with it.

He sat with his head bowed, though, wondering. Was there anything he could have done differently? Beside him, a pair of tartan trews sat on the edge of his desk. He could see a shawl that was worn above them flop onto his desk as well. He looked up and saw Clarissa looking down at him. Her hair was purple again, but it wasn't as long as it had been. She was placing a coffee on his desk.

'Do you want to talk about it?' she asked.

'Yes,' said Patterson.

Chapter 02

Hope McGrath stood in front of the mirror. She'd just stepped out of the shower, and her focus was just below her midriff. It was there now, so much more prominent—the little one, causing her body to bulge. She put her hand down and ran it smoothly across the bulge.

There was no one in the house except herself. A part of her wished John was here. He was finding it a little difficult. Maybe most fathers did. He could see Hope change, could see the tiny life grow inside from the scans she'd been to. He could see the bump develop, but she wanted him to feel the kick. She felt things, movements. So far, he hadn't, but that would come. She wanted John to feel what she felt, but he told her that if that was the case, men would have babies too. She ran her hand across the belly again, and then she thought she felt something. Was that a kick?

Hope was late this morning. She'd phoned in to say she'd be slightly late since she'd been up quite a bit that morning, throwing up. It wasn't getting any easier. As much as she loved having the little one growing inside of her, she could do without this sickness, this insatiable urge to chunder.

It'd been too much that morning, and she'd lain in for another hour before dragging herself into the shower. She dressed now in her pregnancy jeans. They had that elastic band that just was so much more comfortable. Pulling a top on, Hope grabbed her leather jacket.

As she stood at the door, she turned to the hallway mirror. That hair. She went off to find a brush. Hope stood in front of the mirror, brushing away, almost as an indulgence. Her red hair was gleaming. It was crazy how good your hair got just because you had a baby inside. What was that all about? It wasn't like the baby could even see it.

John loved it, though. Her hair was something he seemed to worship. He ran his fingers through it all the time, almost to the point of annoyance some days. And here it was, looking like she was appearing in some sort of conditioner commercial.

By the time Hope made the car, she reckoned she was going to be at least an hour and a half, if not two hours, late by the time to the station. As she arrived, the car park was busy, cars going here and there, and there seemed to be an air of, not excitement, but certainly urgency about the station.

Hope went to walk in the rear door, and it was suddenly thrown open, with several uniformed officers racing out towards their cars. Hope stepped to one side, for they didn't say sorry. They were too focused for that. She walked in and up the steps, making her way to her own office. Arriving, she stared at her team. They were getting things together. Perry was grabbing his coat. Susan was on the phone, but there was an urgency about her, and Ross was on the move.

'Morning, boss,' said Ross. 'Just had a body dumped on the A9.'

'Excuse me?' said Hope. 'A body dumped on the A9?'

'Just north of the bridge.' The bridge Ross was referring to was the Kessock Bridge. It was almost iconic in Inverness. 'It's a bit north of it, just after the turn-off at Munlochy,' said Ross.

'When you say a body dumped . . .?'

'Middle of the road. On my way now.'

'Well, I guess I'm coming with you then,' said Hope.

She looked over at Perry and Susan. 'You two, take the other car. Ross will drive me there.'

Hope spun on her heel and began walking down the stairs. Ross raced past her, out to the car, and when Hope got to it, the door was already open and the engine running. She hauled herself into the passenger seat, belted up and sat back while Ross drove.

'You feeling okay?' asked Ross.

'I feel like crap, Alan, but thank you for asking.'

'I can cover this if you're not—'

'Alan, I talked about this. I'll decide when I'm not able, and I'll let you know. In the meantime, we've got a job to do. Let's go.'

Ross nodded. Hope had found her team becoming more and more protective of her. She guessed it was only normal. After all, they could see the bump developing. She was a woman with a child. And most decent men had an instinct to protect you. As for Susan, you'd have thought she was actually the kid's auntie, the excitement it was generating with her.

'Call came in not long before you arrived. Apparently, the body was dumped onto the road, middle of the A9. We've shut the road. They're sending everyone round from through Munlochy, and up round the back to Tore. So, it's closed off the entire section, both ways.'

'Good,' said Hope. It would cause absolute havoc. There was nothing else you could do about that.

The A9 was a dual, though sometimes single, carriageway

11

that ran through the Highlands and continued going north up towards Wick. The particular section at Inverness was a busy one, and the diversion would take the traffic down through Munlochy, a small village on the Black Isle. There was also a bridge at Munlochy which could only take traffic one way at a time. There'd be hold-ups and complaints, but there was a body. You couldn't have people looking at a body lying in the middle of the road while they were passing by.

The traffic got more congested beyond the bridge. Ross put the police blue lights on, and tore up the hard shoulder. Once they cleared the traffic at the Munlochy turn-off, the road was empty. Ross drove over a summit, to see where the road had been closed off completely. There was a body lying there and Ross pulled up near to it, just outside the scene tapes.

'Do we know if the victim was dead on deposit?' asked Hope.

'Well, Jona's there. Best ask her. She doesn't seem to have covered anything up yet.'

'Probably just here,' said Hope. She walked over to where she saw the forensic wagon and Jona covered from head to foot in the protective clothing for the scene.

'Get some gear on, and you can join me,' said Jona. Hope took her leather jacket off, donned the protective clothing, and then followed Jona out into the middle of the road. Ross stood back at a distance. As they got up close, Hope saw the victim was a middle-aged man.

'Mid-thirties probably,' said Jona, looking at him. Jona knelt down, scanning the man, for he had wounds around his face, and over his body. He was entirely naked.

'He's been beaten,' said Jona.

'I gathered that,' said Hope.

'More than that, he's been tortured. Look!' said Jona, and

pointed down at the man's hands. Two fingernails had been pulled out. There were also stab marks around him, here and there. 'They're not enough to kill, but they'd certainly make you want to ask them to stop. I may be able to get an idea of the blades used. But he's been hit with heavy objects too. Blunt.'

'And he's bound as well,' said Hope. 'Just tossed out the back of a van. You'd need a van, wouldn't you? You couldn't drop him from a car.'

'I don't know the exact details. Best talk to the constables who were here,' said Jona.

'Was he dead before he got here?' asked Hope.

'Give me a minute,' said Jona. She felt the body, looked over at the wounds, and then looked at the surrounding ground.

'I'll confirm it later, but I suspect he was dead when he was dumped here. There's no new bleeding. He's cold—very cold. He'd be warmer than this if he was murdered here, or briefly before he was dumped.'

Hope nodded. She looked at the man, and then felt her hand whip up to her mouth. Damn, she hated this queasiness and the morning sickness.

'Excuse me,' said Hope. She turned and walked away, and Ross went to intercept her. But she put her hand up, disappeared off to the side of the road, before vomiting out of sight. When she came back into view of everyone else, Ross was holding a bottle of water. She thanked him, took it, drank, and washed her mouth out.

'You ever thought of being a maid?' Hope said to Ross. He looked at her, a little annoyed.

'Sorry,' she said. 'It's very kind of you. Jona reckons tortured and beaten. Dumped here. Do we know anything else?'

'That's the sergeant on scene, there,' said Ross, taking Hope over to him. The man was in his late forties and was very grim-faced.

'Report came in,' he said. 'Basically, our drivers came over the summit and saw a van dropping the body.'

'What do you mean by dropping the body?' asked Hope.

'Van, back doors open and literally dumped.'

'We got a license plate for the van?'

'No, not sure there was a number plate. Nobody can remember seeing a number plate. Description of a small white van, basically.'

'How small?'

'Small transit. You could stand up in the back of it, they said.'

'You'd have to, wouldn't you?' said Ross. 'If you're going to dump a body out.'

'Anything else?' asked Hope.

'Nobody was close to the van when it happened. It was like all the traffic came over the top of the hill just to see it.'

'Do you think they wanted us to see it? Do you think—'

'Hold that thought, Ross,' said Hope. She stood looking at the crest of the hill, then down to where the body was. She then turned and walked up to the top.

Standing on the crest, she looked down and then said to Ross, 'Get a bit of paper about the size of a number plate. Write letters on it, the size number plates have. There's a marker pen somewhere in your car, I'm sure of it.'

Ross did so, and then walked down towards the body, stopping a little short of it, and held the paper up. It had letters on it, but Hope was struggling to make them out.

She rejoined Ross. 'It's at a distance, hard to make out the registration. They said it was white, yes?'

'That's what they're saying.'

Perry came over with Susan. 'We've been briefed,' he said. 'What do you want?'

'Go interview the witnesses. I take it the cars that came over the summit are still being held?'

The sergeant nodded.

'Right, Perry, Susan, go over and do that. Get some CCTV. We need to check this white van, where it came from. There should be traffic cameras along here. And Perry, need to get an ID on that man. He's been dropped off by a van. We don't know where the van's come from yet, don't know where it's gone. We don't know who he is. Top priorities, name of that individual, and find the van, or at least where it went.'

Perry nodded, and he and Susan turned away. 'We're going to have the press all over this one, aren't we?' said Ross.

'Too right,' said Hope. 'Let's make sure we keep a tight ring around this. The road's closed. Sergeant, tell them the road's going to be closed the rest of the day. Get traffic to put as good a diversion as they can in place and get people routing away from this. We'll also need some constables up the side. You can come in from the fields here to have a look. I suspect we're going to want the tent over that body soon. It's out in the open. Too easy for anything to fly over. Let's get one of those air traffic zones up around here. I don't want anybody flying over and taking pictures.'

'Why dump a body here?' asked Ross. 'What's the point? Like you say, you've got a load of TV cameras, basic traffic cameras up and down the A9. It's one of the busiest roads going. Why dump it here?'

'Well, it's going to be found,' said Hope.

'It's going to make the news, big time,' said Ross. 'Look at the

15

inconvenience it's caused. This is not just about getting rid of somebody you've killed. They want the body to be found, but they wanted to cause maximum disruption. That's the thing about Inverness, isn't it?'

'How do you mean?'

'Somewhere gets blocked up, it's not that easy to go round it. Whenever you get an accident up here on the bridge, or beyond it, you close traffic going this way. If the back road is out towards Muir of Ord, that jams up traffic, too. You've got to go through the back road through Munlochy now. That's going to get locked up. Everybody's going to know about this body. Everybody's going to know what's going on with it. It's going to be major news. They've done this deliberately.'

'I think you're right,' said Hope. She turned and looked about, trying to see if there was anything else she was missing. 'Just one thing,' she said. 'What was all the fuss going on at the station? Was it for this?'

'No,' said her sergeant. 'We're quite stressed at the moment. This happened, but before that, we'd been on the go for a couple of hours, trying to find a missing child, baby stolen from a pram.'

Hope was not ready for that. Her stomach twisted into a knot. A child taken from a pram. She realised that in the past she would be horrified, as any right-minded adult would be. But now, carrying a child, she could almost feel herself cry. She fought tears back and stiffened up.

'Let's see what we can do here. Clear this as quick as we can, then,' she said to Ross. 'Thorough mind, though. Sounds like our uniformed friends have got a lot on their plate.'

'Of course,' said Ross. He strode off to his duties. Hope McGrath stood alone, pondering the missing child and the dead body. It was going to be a busy day for the Inverness force.

Chapter 03

DCI Seoras Macleod was holding back in his office. He had been keen to get involved too much recently. But then again, the stakes were very different from normal work. The recent events with the secret organisation who had taken out criminals, and those who were perpetrating crimes to highlight this fact, had taken a toll. He'd taken overall charge, moved his pieces and had come up with good solutions. After all, Isabella Isbister, the wife of his colleague who had been killed, was now free from a life of servitude to a new husband she hadn't wanted.

She was away somewhere, looked after by Anna Hunt, the head of the Service. Macleod could get back to ordinary policing. And in that vein, he hadn't rushed out to see the body dumped on the A9. He had Hope for that. That was her job. And as luck would have it, her being pregnant meant that if he reacted too quickly, she would take that as an insult.

He'd also heard about the child who was missing. That always caused an issue. When children were involved, it was hard to keep focused. Hard not to get worked up, hard not to push yourself beyond your limits to a point where your work wasn't as thorough as it could be out of sheer tiredness. He would have to prepare a press statement, though, about the body soon. Take that off of Hope. He would do it, for there would certainly be press. There would be questions. Nothing he couldn't handle. He put on his coat in his office, the fedora hat onto his head, and stepped out. As he turned to walk along, he heard a shout.

'Is that you out, Seoras? Any idea when you're back?'

He turned to see Tanya, his new PA. 'I don't know. If anybody wants me, I'm not available,' said Macleod. 'I'll probably be back before I head up home tonight.'

'Very good,' said Tanya. 'I've got some of that typing you asked for. We've got some timesheets we have to go through as well.'

'It'll keep,' said Macleod.

'Of course,' said Tanya. 'But they will need to be gone through.'

Macleod smiled back at her. 'That's your job to make sure I get them done,' he said. 'You settling in okay?'

'I am. The team's friendly.'

'Just don't let them pull anything past you. You're my defence here. Okay? You work for me, none of them. You're here to protect me in that office.'

'No worries there,' said Tanya. 'In fact . . .'

Macleod was about to turn away, but now he stopped. 'In fact what?' asked Macleod.

'The Assistant Chief Constable was down earlier, asking to see you, but I told him you were busy.'

'When?' asked Macleod.

'Approximately half an hour ago.'

'I was just having my coffee, waiting to go out to Hope. I didn't want to get there too early. Was it important?'

'Well, he didn't say he had to get in to see you. So, I assumed not.'

'Couldn't have been important then,' said Macleod. 'However, with him, make sure you find out. If it's anything to do with manning or timesheets or that, it's not important whatever he says. But he does sometimes need to see me.'

'Of course,' said Tanya. 'I'll make sure that I know.'

Macleod looked at her. She was shrewd, wasn't she? She was an operator within that world. The world of paperwork, meetings, and all the rest. A world that Macleod wasn't an operator in. That's why he needed a secretary to protect him.

'Don't hang about for me,' said Macleod. 'If you're done, go. I'll be fine. Besides, you need to get yourself sorted with accommodation. Make sure you settle in properly.'

'Of course. Speak to you later.'

Macleod made his way down the stairs, out to his car in the car park. He could feel the busyness of the station. The child still hadn't been found, and part of him always felt the drag to get involved. To say he could spare a few hours to help but really there were other DCIs who were better placed to do that.

Macleod drove past the traffic and fought his way through to the closed off section of the A9. On arrival, he sought Hope, seeing the red-hair ponytail from a distance. He walked up behind her, tapping her on the shoulder, and she spun.

'What?' she said. 'Oh sorry, it's you.'

'Yes, it's me,' said Macleod. 'Just coming for an update, seeing as I hadn't received one.'

'The road's closed; there's a body on it,' said Hope.

Macleod could sense she was busy, and possibly not getting that far. She also looked tired.

'Is sickness still a problem?' he said.

She looked around quickly, and then turned back to him, aware that no one was close. 'Yes, sickness is a bloody problem,' said Hope. 'People need to stop going on about it. I said, when it becomes an issue, I'll withdraw. Till then—'

'Okay,' said Macleod. He watched her turn away, looking over towards where the body was now covered by a large tent.

'What do we know?' he asked.

'Well, Jona's checked the body over. Hopefully, we can reopen the road soon. The forensics complete. She says she's stretched, though.'

'Missing child. Anything on that yet?'

'I haven't heard anything from the station. Certainly haven't found the wee mite. If they'd found him, everybody would know, one way or the other. Jona did find a receipt on our body.'

'A receipt?' said Macleod. 'I heard he was found naked.'

'He was found naked. In his hand was a receipt.'

'Hang on,' said Macleod. 'Did somebody not say that the man was beaten?'

'He was beaten. He was gently knifed, as Jona put it, so as not to kill him, but to torture him.'

'And he was then found with a receipt in his hand? Why would you have a receipt in your hand? He's not held on to this through torture, has he?'

'Jona says it was stuffed in afterwards,' replied Hope. 'Perry's off with it. It's for a local supermarket. He's got a receipt, so he may have been filmed. They do that on the automatic tills, don't they? Especially if it's a self-checkout.'

'So I'm told,' said Macleod. 'I don't use them.'

'Keeping somebody in a job or not able to work them?'

Macleod raised an eyebrow. 'I'm perfectly capable of

21

working them,' he said. 'Just choose not to.' It was a lie, but he would not admit that.

'Ross has got on to the CCTV. There are the basic traffic cameras up and down. Not for speed, just to monitor the traffic passing by. They've got a number plate as it left the scene, but he says he can't find it coming in, though. The number plate's false. He's checked it. Reckons there's a man driving it. But it's not clear. He's also wearing a mask, by the looks of it.

'I don't know if the number plates were changed close to the scene. We can't find the van arriving, just departing. It left straight away after dumping the body but then vanishes from the surrounding cameras in the area. Lot more searching to do though, Ross says. There are other white vans, though but they have different number plates. We're going to see if we can match things up. But it's early days with that.'

'Why not just burn the van out once you get away?' pondered Macleod.

'That would seem the obvious solution,' said Hope. 'Destroy it.'

'Unless you need it again,' said Macleod.

Hope stared at him. 'Need it again?'

'Just a thought. Anyway, what else do we know?'

'Susan's been talking to the people who saw the body being dumped. There were a couple of drivers who came over the summit as the body was thrown out of the back and the white van pulled away. They were the ones who called the police in the first place. The van slowed down, but didn't stop. Our witnesses reckon two men were dumping the body out of the rear of the van. You probably wouldn't need two people if you were going to push him out.'

22

'So you've got at least three people associated with the van?'

'There's only one in the front seats, which means when it comes out the other side,' said Hope, 'like most white vans it will have one person driving. Most don't have two in the front seats. Usually delivery drivers, isn't it?'

'Okay. So, you're using the CCTV to trace the van. But no license plate numbers.'

'We're hoping to get lucky by finding the van again on CCTV and getting the real number plate. We haven't got a description of the driver because it's too far away. And he's not showing up in the cameras because we think he's wearing a mask.'

'Got anything about the van we can go on?' asked Macleod.

'Some tyre tracks a little way before on the side of the road. Right into the muck off the hard shoulder. Van could have gone in there. It would have been out of sight to most people driving past. Could change your number plates there.'

'Okay, so you should get the tyre print. It's going to be a lot to find all the white vans and check their tyre prints, though,' said Macleod. 'More a thing for the courts, eventually.'

'Doing what we can,' said Hope. 'But if you think about it, if they were going to dump the body, they'd need a gap to do that. You wouldn't just drive down and dump it with everybody driving past you. You could get seen. As I said, the distance from the top of the hill,' said Hope, 'down to the body, meant that they couldn't identify the men dumping the body out. I think it's deliberate. They're waiting for a gap, so they may have waited in there.'

'So, your CCTV's going to go back at least, what, ten minutes, fifteen, half an hour before the arrival here?'

'Well, who knows how long?' said Hope.

Macleod looked around him. Everyone was busy. He stood

and tried to get a feel for the murder, how it happened.

'I don't get it either,' said Hope. 'But Ross said something to me. He said that they wanted people to know. The body being dumped here causes major traffic problems. It's big news.'

'Body brought here,' said Macleod. 'He was killed elsewhere, yes?'

'Jona thinks so. Thinks he was dead before he got here.'

'So, killed him somewhere else, then brought him here. So this is important. Causes major traffic problems. That could be the reason. There's nothing particular I can see about the road here. It's like any other piece of road. Farmland around it. I'm not getting it. Why here, as a location? Other than for the traffic,' said Macleod.

'Been pondering that too,' said Hope. 'I can't find any other reason. Other than they want it to be news. Want it to be a big thing.'

Macleod nodded but he wasn't happy. As Macleod stood, he heard the vibration of Hope's phone from her pocket and watched as she picked it up, stepping away for a moment.

'It's Hope. Really? Wow. Okay. Are you sure about that? Got an image for me? If you have, can you send it to us? Appreciate that.'

Macleod looked over at her when she'd finished the phone call. 'So, something new,' he said.

'That was Perry. He's been down to the supermarket. The man paid for the goods at a conventional till, but he says the credit card used was for a Kevin MacTavish.'

'Okay. Should I know Kevin? Kevin MacTavish?' asked Macleod.

'No,' said Hope, 'but Uniform are currently looking for Kevin MacTavish regarding the missing child. Perry's getting some

CCTV imagery. He's going to try to coordinate the cameras with the purchase, get us a face, and then we'll see MacTavish— see if anybody recognises him.'

'Makes sense,' said Macleod, 'go and see if they are tied in. Bit of a coincidence, have your body dumped while the child is taken. Who's Kevin MacTavish regarding the child?'

'He's the uncle of the child that's missing.'

'Really? He's the uncle?'

'Don't like this,' said Hope. 'Missing child and dead body doesn't bode well.'

'No, it doesn't,' said Macleod. 'But let's not jump to conclusions. Let's just take it as it comes, okay?'

'Okay,' Hope nodded. 'Okay, once we're all sorted here, I'll head over to see the MacTavishes.'

'I'll come with you,' said Macleod. 'There'll be a lot of noise around the missing child. To get some decent access, it'll be best if the two of us go.'

'Yes,' said Hope. 'I was going to ask you to, anyway.'

'Are you okay?' asked Macleod.

'You know how you feel when it's a missing child or a child that's involved in the murder?'

'Of course,' said Macleod.

'See, when you carry one, Seoras, it's ten times worse.'

Macleod nodded and watched as Hope stood sucking the air in deeply. 'Still, it needs done. Let's go.'

Chapter 04

Macleod and Hope parked up outside a council estate house on the edge of Inverness. There were several marked police cars outside it, as well as some that weren't marked. Macleod could see neighbours peering out of their houses to see who was arriving. That was the thing about a missing child. Everybody wanted to know what was going on. Everybody was concerned, keen to help.

There was also the selfish interest, the curiosity of people. That wasn't always pleasant to behold.

Macleod made his way to the front door, which was opened for him by a young officer, who recognised him immediately. Hope followed in behind him. She wondered if her appearance would affect the woman. A pregnant woman standing there, reminding her what she'd lost. However, she couldn't help that. But maybe that was why Macleod had offered to come too. He could always order Hope to do something, if the situation called for it, with no one losing face.

They were shown into the living room of the house, where a young blonde-haired woman was clearly distressed on the sofa. She'd been crying, judging by the look of her eyes, which were heavy and leaden. Her hair was in a mess too, and she'd clearly been sweating from fear, maybe from anxiety.

A liaison officer was sitting close by, but there was another woman sitting there. She had brown hair, and her name was Anne Lewis. The liaison officer introduced her as Tommy MacTavish's pseudo-aunt, the partner of Kevin MacTavish.

'My apologies for disturbing you at such a difficult time,' said Macleod. 'It's not actually you I need to talk to, Emma. I need to talk to Anne, if you don't mind.'

'It's maybe best if we speak outside,' said Hope. She could see Emma looking at her, clearly able to identify that Hope was pregnant.

'Stay,' said Emma, reaching over to Anne. 'Surely you can talk about whatever it is here.'

'Well, if you must,' said Macleod. 'I'm afraid it might upset you as well, Emma.'

'What else can you tell me that would upset me?' she blurted.

Macleod took a deep breath and then reached for his phone and pulled up an image that had been taken from the supermarket CCTV.

'I'd like you to look at this person on the phone, Anne, and tell me, do you recognise him?'

Anne took the phone off Macleod. Instantly, her face showed she recognised the man. And she looked up at Macleod. 'Is he all right?'

'Who is it?' asked Macleod.

'It's, well, it's Kevin.'

'It's Kevin?' Emma said. 'Why have you got a photograph of Kevin?'

'I'm afraid to tell you both that Kevin is dead.'

He watched as the women went white. And then Anne shook her head. 'No. No, no. He's not.'

'I'm afraid he is,' said Macleod. 'I'm sorry for your loss.'

'What do you mean?' screamed Emma. 'What do you mean, he's dead? How can our Kevin be dead?'

'Kevin was found dead on the A9,' said Macleod.

'A car accident?' said Anne, fighting back tears.

'No,' said Macleod. 'I'm afraid someone murdered Kevin.'

'What?' shouted Emma. 'Someone murdered Kevin? You're wrong!'

'Enought, it's exactly as I say,' said Macleod. 'I'm sorry, but Kevin was murdered, and his body was left on the A9 today.'

Anne sunk back into her seat. She was shaking her head. 'It can't be,' she said. 'Can't be.'

'Sorry, but it is,' said Macleod.

'There's some mistake,' said Anne suddenly, defiant. 'Kevin had gone to meet someone to purchase something for work. That's what he said. He'd gone to meet someone to purchase something for work. It won't be him.'

'Where does Kevin work?' asked Macleod.

'Lord Bairstow's estate; it's—'

'It's west of Inverness,' said Hope, 'near Contin, yes?'

'Yes, yes,' said Anne, 'but he's at work. He was going to work this morning, but he had to pick up this purchase for work.'

'Where was the purchase being made?' asked Hope.

'I don't know,' said Anne. 'I have no idea. He just told me he had to pick something up before getting into work. If they called, I was just to tell them that, that's what he was doing.'

'Never mind,' said Emma. 'I mean, we can't do anything for him now. But Tommy's still out there. Tommy's alive. Tommy is—'

'Yes, he is,' said Macleod. 'We have people out looking for him. But I need to know about Kevin. It may not be related—it may. I have no idea as of yet,' said Macleod.

'Get out and look for Tommy!' screamed Emma.

'We have nearly everyone out looking for Tommy,' said Macleod. 'We are searching.'

'It's a missing child,' said Hope. 'The entire force will push their hours, will pull out all the stops for a child. Doesn't matter what time, whatever. They'll put extra hours in. Everyone will look for Tommy,' said Hope.

Emma burst into tears again, and the police liaison woman comforted her.

'Anne,' said Macleod, 'does Kevin normally do this?'

'Sometimes. Sometimes he goes elsewhere to pick stuff up for work. But this one was very last minute. That's why he was telling me. Normally, he wouldn't bother. He'd taken a call, and he said to me he had to nip off before work.'

'So work was aware, then?' asked Hope.

'Well,' she said, 'I received a call from his work a little later. They asked where he was.'

'And what did you say to them?' asked Macleod.

'I said what Kevin had said to tell them. That he'd gone off to pick up this purchase.'

'How did they react?' asked Macleod.

'Well, they were . . . they seemed a little bemused. But they didn't . . . they didn't make a fuss of it. They just, well . . . they just sort of said okay.'

'So you think they weren't aware?' asked Macleod.

'It's a big place,' said Anne. 'Maybe that person wasn't aware. Maybe they went to ask. I don't know.' Then she stopped and looked at Macleod again. 'Dead? Murdered?'

'I'm afraid so,' said Macleod. 'He'd gone to the supermarket on the way past to wherever he was going. He'd bought a can and a sandwich, I think,' said Macleod. 'He was found with the receipt. That's why we could get the photograph. It was attached to his credit card as well. The name, with what had happened with Tommy, the surname stuck out. So that's how we found you. I'm terribly sorry,' said Macleod. 'Do you know if Kevin was in any trouble?'

'Kevin? No,' said Anne.

'Kevin just wanted to be a big uncle to Tommy. Kevin's good,' said Emma. 'Do you understand? Why would somebody kill Kevin? Why would you do that? Why would you—'

'I don't know yet,' said Macleod. 'I will find out.'

'Find my Tommy,' said Emma, beginning to cry again. 'Find my Tommy.'

'Can you give me details of Kevin's car?' asked Macleod. 'Details of friends, contacts. We'll pop along and see his work. We'll inform them so you don't have to bother with those connections.'

They spent the next ten minutes getting names from Anne of who Kevin's friends were. Once they'd done that, Macleod again said he was sorry for their trouble, and he would find out who had done this. As they stepped outside, Hope tapped Macleod on the shoulder.

'Gone off to get something for work, but work doesn't seem to know about it.'

'Certainly, some of work doesn't seem to know about it,' said Macleod. 'But then, they're bemused, but they don't question it any further.'

'You would ask, wouldn't you?' said Hope. 'Ask what it was. Ask who had sent him.'

'You would think so.'

'You'd think they'd make some sort of fuss.'

'We need to speak then to them. Find his boss. See what was

going on.'

The pair slipped into the car but before Macleod drove off, Hope's phone rang.

'This is Hope.'

'This is Perry again. Did we get our man?'

'We did. What's up, Perry?'

'We're looking through the CCTV. We got the van departing, but we can't find it after a couple of miles. So we've tried to do a search pattern to see if we can find it hidden away.'

'Any sign of it arriving on scene yet?'

'Nothing. All the white vans that come through before it, they've got their registration plate, and we've checked where they are, and they're all legit. Most of them aren't quite the same size. That's the thing about white vans. You think they're all the same, but they're not. They're different. Different designs. Slight differences. It's slow going, but, well, we might get there soon.'

'Our man Kevin,' said Hope, 'was off on an errand. He works for Lord Bairstow, west of Inverness, out Contin way. The boss and I are going out there now. See what's—'

Macleod put his hand up. 'No,' he said, 'take Ross with you.'

'Why?' asked Hope.

'You're the DI and the investigating officer. I came here to help in a delicate situation, pregnant lady meeting a woman whose child's been kidnapped. You don't need me out there. Take Ross. A DCI turning up on the doorstep might look a bit much.'

'Okay,' said Hope, but her face clearly showed she thought Macleod was up to something or had other reasons he wasn't sharing.

'I'm going to come and pick up Ross,' continued Hope. 'How

31

far is Jona from opening up the A9?'

'She's got the tyre tracks. No matches for it yet, but we're doing our best. We did go through all the other vans that we've found so far. None of their tyre tracks match.'

'Good,' said Hope. 'Keep at it. The more you can eliminate, the better. Don't be afraid to stretch the time clock out. See how many other vans arrived before that. It could have hidden in there for a while.'

'Will do,' said Perry. She closed down the call, put the phone away, and Macleod started the car.

'Are you okay?' he asked.

'Told you before, stop going on about it. It's just morning sickness.'

'No,' said Macleod, 'not that. You're carrying a kid. There's a kid missing. It looks like this case could tie into it. Are you going to be okay?'

'In what way?' asked Hope. 'You think I'm going to buckle because I've got Junior on board?'

'Don't do that,' said Macleod. 'I get worked up. I don't have kids. Never had kids. I get worked up around small ones whenever they're involved in any of this. You're carrying one. You're a mum. I've seen the way Ross goes around things with children. I'm looking out for you. Are you going to be okay?'

'I think so,' said Hope. 'I won't lie to you, Seoras. The morning sickness thing is hard. But I've got to be better than that. I've got to deal with it, you know.'

'No, I don't,' said Macleod. 'I'm not putting that pressure on you. If you need to go off sick because maternity is doing this to you? Fine. You won't get an argument out of me. Come back when you're ready.'

'You don't understand, do you?' said Hope. 'I'm a career

woman. I can't be seen to be backing off.'

'Why?' said Macleod. He said it gently, like he did when he needed you to hear his point.

Hope didn't have an answer for that. She thought she needed to look as strong as a man. She needed to show that the career would not stop because she was having a baby. But she knew Macleod wouldn't care about that. She turned and looked out the window.

'Just be careful,' said Macleod. 'The stuff we get involved with, sometimes it bites on you. And it bites on you hard. Watch your judgment? Stick to your role.'

'Yes, sir,' she said. She was looking out the window, deep in thought about the wee one inside her and how Emma must be feeling. The sickness in the morning and the queasiness, they were nothing. But the feelings she had now, knowing what Emma was going through—that was harder than any amount of vomiting ever was.

Chapter 05

Macleod dropped Hope back at the station, where, on returning to her office, she found Ross awaiting her. Susan was sitting with Perry, going through CCTV footage, and Hope said she would see them when she got back. Ross grabbed his jacket, and in his car, they made their way out towards Lord Bairstow's estate.

They headed out on the Ullapool road, towards Contin, and the estate that was just to the west of it. Lord Bairstow's estate had a large wall around most of it, but it also had a manned front gate with just the one person.

The guard who was there said that Lord Bairstow was in. He would ring ahead to say that they were coming. Hope looked up at a large building further beyond. As far as stately homes went, it wasn't particularly grand, but it was large—more functional than impressive. The driveway up to it swept left and right before arriving at a large area to the front of the building where several cars were parked. Ross found a space and together they walked up to the looming front doors. Ross rapped on it with the large brass knocker attached to the door.

Hope looked around because the light was failing, and she felt a little tired. Today hadn't started well, and taking on the case was exhausting. She also hadn't eaten properly. She'd have to do that after this. Make Ross take her somewhere. The trouble was, it wasn't as if she was on full steam. Even then, cases were exhausting. But if she didn't eat in her current state, the energy would sap away from her. Not surprising. She was growing a life, after all.

One of the large wooden doors was pulled back and what could only be described as a butler stepped out to greet them. Hope removed her warrant card and presented it to the man.

'DI Hope McGrath. This is DS Alan Ross. We'd like to speak to Lord Bairstow, or someone connected with his estate, if possible. It's regarding a Kevin MacTavish.'

'Young Kevin? Of course. I'll inform Lord Bairstow you're here. I hope everything's okay.'

'Well, I'd rather speak to Lord Bairstow about that,' said Hope. The butler asked them to follow him, took them inside, and they were seated in a rather stately hall. He returned two minutes later.

'Lord Bairstow will see you in the drawing room. This way, please.'

Hope and Ross followed the man along a corridor, and then into a large, wood-panelled room. There was a chaise lounge and a couple of sofas, along with a writing desk. Wood was on every wall, only covered by large family portraits.

'His Lordship will see you in here. I've been asked if I can get you anything in the meantime.'

'I'm fine,' said Hope. Ross indicated so too, and the man left. Approximately, a minute later, a door on the far side of the room opened up, and a man walked in. He was wearing a tweed suit, with a shirt underneath which was laid open at the collar.

'Sorry to keep you waiting,' said a rather jovial man. He

had a moustache and grey hair but was bald on top. He was definitely rotund, and Hope thought he looked like the grand old lord.

'Lord Bairstow, I presume,' said Hope, once again pulling out her warrant card, but the man waved it away.

'My man said DI McGrath and this will be your sergeant, Ross, wasn't it?'

'Yes, sir,' said Ross.

'I have some bad news for you,' said Hope, but the man walked towards her suddenly.

'Ah, I see you've got some good news yourself. Can I offer you a seat? Please, don't feel you have to stand around me.' He turned and rang a bell, and the same butler arrived back. 'Get the inspector here a, what, orange juice? A glass of water? A cup of tea? I've got decaf coffee if you like.'

'I'm absolutely fine, sir.'

'Nonsense,' said Bairstow. 'Absolute nonsense. Bring a jug of water with ice and some cups and a glass for the Inspector. Ross, what would you like? Get you a whisky, man?'

'I'm on duty, sir,' said Ross. 'If you insist, I'll take a coffee.'

'Of course, I insist. Grab a seat, too. You don't need to stand and be formal. Please, sit, Inspector.' Hope was going to challenge him, but in truth, she was tired, and getting off her feet was a good idea. The water would be welcome.

'I'll take a double whisky, James,' he said to the butler.

'Very good, sir. I shall return directly.' The man turned on his heel and walked out the door.

'Sorry,' said Bairstow, pulling up a chair alongside the sofa that Hope was now sitting on. 'You said you had some disturbing news.'

'I'm afraid I have to inform you that Kevin MacTavish, one

of your workers, is dead.'

Bairstow seemed to think for a moment. 'MacTavish? Kevin? Ah! Wasn't in today, was he? Oh. Oh, that is bad news. If one can ask, how did it happen?'

'That's the rather disturbing bit, sir. You may have read on the news about the road being closed on the A9. Well, that was because of a body that was found there.'

'Yes, the news said something about that.'

'Well, the body was Kevin MacTavish,' said Hope.

'My, my, tragic.'

'Do you work with him directly, sir?' asked Ross.

'No, but, well, this might be rather indelicate . . .'

'You have information about him,' said Ross.

'Well, one doesn't like to say,' said Bairstow, 'but I guess considering the circumstances, I should tell all.'

'Please do,' said Hope. Bairstow was about to speak when the door opened and the butler came in with a tray. He pulled a table close to Hope and placed a jug of iced water, along with a glass, beside her before pouring her some. He then lifted a coffee off for Ross before handing Lord Bairstow a double whisky.

'Will that be all, sir?'

'Yes. Thank you, James,' said Bairstow. He waited until the butler had left, and then took a sip of his whisky, before looking back over at Hope. 'Kevin didn't come in today. The staff called when he didn't come in just to see if he was all right. You know, it's what you do nowadays. One doesn't phone them up and ask them where the hell they are. You phone them up and say, are you okay? One's doing the same thing at the end of the day, trying to find out what's gone on. Well, then they phoned up. He wasn't there. And his, I think it's his partner, said that Kevin had gone off to pick up a package. Well, the staff knew nothing about that.'

'Are you aware of any package, sir?' asked Ross.

'There's been no package, no meeting up with anyone. I do not know where he was going for what. It's not to do with his work here. What we know was that, well, Kevin's very fond of Lauren, Lauren Starr. She's one of my employees. She's an office worker.'

'Here on the estate?' asked Hope.

'Yes. Yes, Lauren works here, and, well, Kevin would have seen her daily in his work. He didn't work directly with her, but he certainly would have passed her by multiple times a day. Would have been on speaking terms with her in any case. Would have had to see her about the odd thing. The thing is, Lauren, great worker, absolutely no problems with her work, but she could be a distraction.'

'How do you mean?' asked Hope.

'Not her fault,' said Bairstow. 'Sometimes when you employ many people, you get to know this. But I took Lauren on because, well, you have to. She had all the qualifications. Excellent person. But, well, she was twenty-three, and she had some looks about her. Bit like yourself,' said Bairstow.

Hope almost felt resentful at first. She didn't like being referred to as the good-looking one. She was a detective first and foremost. But she'd got used to people seeing her in that way, certainly men. Not all, but a good quantity of them.

'Was she particularly looking out for men, or did she like to be seen?'

'No,' said Bairstow, 'not at all. Lauren dressed sensibly, modern, but you know what the modern outfits are like. Tight fitting, so her curves were there to be seen, and she attracted attention, and I'm afraid to say I think Kevin really did rather like her.'

'To what degree?' asked Ross.

'Well, the staff all knew various rumours about the two of them being involved with each other. But nothing happened here at work, so it wasn't something to be investigated as such. What people do during the time outside of my employ is up to them if they are discreet about it. If they were not bringing any disrepute onto the firm here, that's fine. It's their life; it's their business, isn't it? But certainly, the two of them were rumoured to be very close.'

'What does this have to do with his death today?' asked Hope.

'Well that's the thing. Lauren wasn't in today either. Lauren called up and said she was ill. I'm not one to cast aspersions,' said Bairstow, and he laughed. 'Not with my background. I've, well, I've dabbled here and there myself, so I'm not turning round and trying to make out I'm holier than thou and condemning them for their actions. But, well, I was once told you don't shit on your own doorstep.'

'I'm sorry?' said Hope.

'I think what Lord Bairstow means,' said Ross, 'is you don't do it at work.'

'Exactly, my man,' said Bairstow. 'If you're going to be doing things like that, do it away from work. Do it away from prying eyes. I'm afraid that they didn't, and that's why the rumours start. And today, they were both off work at the same time. Not good. I would have probably brought them in when they came back and had a word. A quiet word, just to say that it was noted. And with the rumours and that, we certainly don't want to be confirming anything. However, now that he's dead, that would seem to be, well, not something that was going to happen. I'd call ahead and tell Lauren, but I think you probably want to speak to her first, don't you?'

'Absolutely. I'd advise that you don't call her at all,' said Hope. 'Maybe tomorrow after we've spoken to her tonight. Would you have an address for her?'

'Of course,' said Bairstow, and rang a small bell. Thirty seconds later, the butler came. 'James, get me an address for Lauren Starr. It's not far from here, is it?'

'No,' said James. 'As I recall, Little Scatwell.'

Hope looked over at Ross, who shook his head. Bairstow caught the look.

'It's a tiny clump of houses to the west of the estate. Very discreet, you see. You could never see them without going there. I do hope she's okay. You said he was found dead. Was he hit by a car or something?'

'I'm afraid to say he was murdered,' said Hope. 'Probably beaten and tortured. Do you have a phone number for Lauren?'

James hadn't left the room. He turned and left to come back a minute later, clutching a piece of paper.

Hope waved the man over and took the paper off him. She dialled the number on it. It rang, then an answer machine kicked in.

'The answer machine,' said Hope.

'Well, it could just be she's out. Maybe they weren't meeting at all,' said Bairstow.

'Or maybe she's got spooked,' said Ross. 'Or maybe she's involved. We'll have to find out.'

'Of course,' said Hope.

She took a long drink of water. She went to move, but Bairstow was over, taking her hand and lifting her up. 'May I ask how many months?'

'Five,' said Hope.

'Five months. Wow! Beginning to feel then. Are there any kicks?'

Hope smiled. 'Yes,' she said.

'Well, I hope you keep well through it, and all the best with it,' said Bairstow. 'If you need any other help from me, by all means, do advise. If you need statements from the workers here regarding the phone conversation and that, please just come in. We'll make time for you, obviously.'

'Well, that's very understanding of you, sir,' said Hope. She went to leave and then realised that she knew which door she'd come in, but she wasn't quite sure how she'd get back to the front door. Bairstow recognised instantly what was going on.

'I shall see you to the door. It's not a problem,' he said, downing the rest of his whisky.

'I'd like to say it's been a pleasure to meet you,' he said, 'but given the circumstances, maybe we should be a little more contrite.'

He opened the door and let Hope walk through, followed by Ross, before closing it behind him and following them out to the front door. By the time they were standing on the large doorstep, night had fallen.

'Are you okay to get there?' asked Bairstow. 'We can get one of the lads to run you over, show you the way in a Land Rover if you need it.'

'No,' said Hope. 'We should be all right but thank you for your help.'

'If she's there,' said Bairstow, 'I would break it to her gently. I think they were fond of each other. Like I said, it was nothing to do with the business, nothing to do with us, but they always seemed to be keen on each other. And frankly, I don't blame him. Lovely girl. You don't get lucky that often.'

'How do you mean?' asked Hope.

'Beautiful face, beautiful body, beautiful soul,' said Bairstow. Then he laughed a bit. 'I hit the jackpot with my wife. Screwed it up, completely, over some daft filly of a thing. She had no soul. I just went for her because of the looks. My wife at that stage, like us all, was somewhat older than when she was in her prime. The looks come and go, but the soul doesn't. Having a kind soul beside you is everything, don't you think?'

'Well, my Angus is both of those,' said Ross.

Hope saw the vaguest flicker in Bairstow's eyes, and then suddenly the man was laughing. 'Well, look at you, Sergeant Ross,' he said.

'Thanks again,' said Hope. 'If I need you, I'll be in contact.'

'At your service, ma'am,' said Bairstow. He stayed there watching them get into the car and then leave, off to look for Little Scatwell.

Chapter 06

Perry sat looking at the screen. By now, every car that was going past looked the same. They clearly weren't, but he'd seen so many cars, so often going past the same stretches of road, that his eyes were swimming. Beside him, Susan Cunningham seemed to do a lot better. She would point vehicles out to Perry. He would write where they were, what time they were at, what section of road.

They traced many vans and then had sent out uniform to find out if they were at the correct addresses according to the registrations. All had come through, and so far, they were back to square one. They had a vehicle that left the area, but under a false number plate. A white van. They had no image of it arriving.

There wasn't the same vehicle, in and then out. They'd already gone back through the four hours beforehand, and Perry thought it was getting ridiculous now. How long would somebody wait for a gap in the traffic to drop a body off? Of course, Kevin MacTavish had been alive that morning. So, they couldn't go too far back. Four hours was about the limit.

'Do you want more coffee?' asked Susan.

'Please,' said Perry. He sat back, looking at the screen for a moment. But then turned his head after Susan had got up from the chair. He watched her walk all the way to the coffee. Her jeans were tight around her hips and her long blonde hair bounced around her back. It was no longer in a ponytail, for she'd let it out an hour ago. It was her way of trying to ease away the aches and pains of sitting in a seat searching the CCTV. He liked her hair when it was out. It was quite something.

'Hello. Forgot where I live?'

Perry snapped back suddenly and looked in front of him. Above his computer screen was the face of a woman he'd known down in Glasgow, and most recently, who he'd worked with undercover.

'Tanya,' he said. Had she been watching him? He suddenly went a little red.

'Have you seen DCI Macleod?' asked Tanya.

'We usually refer to him as the big boss,' said Perry, trying to give a little laugh and break the moment.

'Have you seen him?' asked Tanya.

Perry shook his head. 'I thought he went out with Hope.'

'He did,' said Tanya. 'I was wondering if he'd come back.'

'You haven't met yet, have you?' said Perry suddenly. 'Susan, this is Tanya. Macleod's secretary.'

'PA,' said Tanya. 'I do a little more than type.'

'Pleased to meet you,' said Susan. 'Would you like a coffee? I was just making Perry one.'

'No, no, I can't stay,' she said. Susan came over with a mug of coffee and put it in front of Perry.

'DC Susan Cunningham, you two work together,' said Tanya.

'We have for a while now,' said Susan. 'Perry, well, Perry saved my life once. I lost a leg.' Susan moved her leg to one side from behind the table and tapped it. She pulled up her jeans and the false foot and metal pole of her false leg could be seen.

'Really?' said Tanya. 'How brave of him.'

'It was,' said Susan. 'The building was falling down and Perry rushed in to get me out.'

Tanya seemed to nod.

'What brings you up from Glasgow?' Susan asked Tanya.

'Well, the big boss, as Perry tells me I have to call him, was looking for a new PA. His last one went off with cancer. Wasn't coming back. I worked down in Glasgow and knew Perry there. Perry sort of recommended me to him.'

'That was nice of you, Perry,' said Susan.

'I was just wondering if you mind if I borrowed Perry for a moment. I've just got a few questions I need to ask him.'

'Oh right,' said Susan. 'By all means, or I can step out if you want. Or, you know, if it's not personal, talk here. We could do with a brief break from this.'

'No, no,' said Perry. 'I'll go outside with Tanya. We'll just have a quick word.'

Tanya turned on her heel and walked out of the office. She had a skirt on that ran past her knees, but it was tight around her hips. For her age, she had an excellent figure, and she was quite happy to show it in a modest sort of way. Nothing flashy, just class, as she thought. Behind, Perry was in two minds. He wondered just why Tanya was bringing him out. Was she worried about Susan? But the mere fact she was, was something quite wonderful as well.

Once she stepped out into the corridor, Tanya turned, and Perry almost walked into her.

'I came up here. You said there was a chance.'

'I've been a tad busy,' said Perry. 'Haven't even thought about

45

that type of thing.'

'Susan in there—is she the competition?' asked Tanya.

Tanya had always been direct. It was something Perry liked about her. She was no nonsense, formidable. That's why she would be good for Macleod. You wouldn't get past Tanya without good reason.

'She's a colleague. She told me to keep my distance before.'

'Before,' said Tanya. 'Sounds good. It seems like there's something coming after before.'

'Well,' said Perry. 'I'll admit, I was very keen on her. But she wasn't—'

'Before. Is she keen now?'

'I don't know,' said Perry.

'Is she keen now? Do you think she's keen now?'

'I can't tell these things. You know what I'm like.'

'I know what you're like, Warren Perry. I know you damn well. And you understand people. If she has given you a rebuttal, and you're now still thinking about it, she has done something else. You wouldn't think otherwise. You're too clever for that.'

'Well, I have done nothing. I haven't sought to—'

'No, but you work together. And is she showing you affection? Is she showing you—'

Perry looked around the corridor. 'Keep it quieter.'

'There's no one about. She won't hear us in there. I'm not daft, Perry.'

'I know you're not daft. That's why I asked you up here.'

'I thought you asked me up here because there was a hope, a chance for us.'

'There is a chance for us.'

'So what? She's just being kept in the wings in case it doesn't work out?'

'Tanya,' said Perry. 'Look . . .' He failed to speak his mind. Perry wasn't very good with matters of the heart. He was better at showing how he felt, not explaining it.

Tanya stepped forward. She grabbed Perry by the collar of his shirt, pulling his face close to hers. 'If she is after you, if she wants you, she is in for a fight.' Tanya planted a kiss on the side of Perry's cheek. 'She's not getting you easy.'

Tanya stepped back and turned. 'If you see DCI Macleod, ask him to drop by his office. Tell him I want him.'

'Of course,' said Perry. But the man was reeling. Tanya had left, and he was still standing in the corridor. She wanted him. Was this not what Perry had wanted? To be wanted? To have someone he was prepared to drop it all for?

Susan popped her head out of the office. 'Everything all right?' she said.

'Fine. She was just asking about a few things. Talking about a few people we used to know.'

'I need you to come in,' said Susan. 'I think I've seen something. I think I saw the van.'

'What?' said Perry. 'How did we miss it?'

'Ten minutes before the body is dumped. It's there.'

'Where? I saw nothing. We scoured that time frame for ages,' said Perry. Susan grabbed Perry's hand and led him back into the office.

'Sit down,' she said. 'Look.'

He looked at the time stamp on the video, and it was about ten minutes before the body had been dumped.

'There,' she said.

'Where?' said Perry.

'There!' Susan pointed at a vehicle. It was a van, and it had a large blue wave running up one side and across the roof, making it almost half blue and half white.

'That's not it. It's not a white van, is it? They said it was a white van. The doors, when they closed it, they said were white. Look at that,' said Perry. And he ran the video on. 'Back doors. They've got blue on them, that blue-wave thing.'

'Look at the shape of the van,' said Susan. 'Look at the wheels. Same type of wheels. Same shape of van. And I mean exactly the same shape of van. I did some measuring with the tools. That van is the same size. Same dimensions across the back. Same style. That van is the same as the one that was seen afterwards when the video was departing. Except it's got a large blue wave running around it. We've got the same vans. It's ten minutes before. It's perfect timing. Get in there. Wait for that big gap.'

'How do they know when a sizeable gap is coming?' said Perry.

'That's easy, is it?' said Susan. 'You have somebody sitting further back in a car of their own on the phone saying, now's your big gap, get out and do it.'

'Well, they're not going to believe that, are they?' said Perry. 'Blue wave van, suddenly a white van.'

'We need to check the bins along the route and just after.'

'What?' said Perry.

'Bins. You don't paint a blue wave van like that, do you? They're decals. They're applied to vehicles. You can take them off.'

'You're telling me they went to the trouble of putting decals all over this van, then parked it up on the side out of the way, whipped them all off, and then drove?'

'I'm not telling you. It's a theory. And I think those decals will be somewhere.'

'Well, the last we see them is before the Munlochy turnoff. In fact, it's just before the turnoff for North Kessock,' said Susan. 'So, they could have pulled in at North Kessock, or on the other side, going onto the Black Isle proper. Or they could have pulled off where we got the tyre tracks.'

'Okay,' said Perry. 'You want to have a look? We'll go and have a look. But I'm honestly not seeing this as a runner. Surely people would have seen them ripping this stuff off.'

'Trust me.'

'I do,' said Perry. 'We'll go out and have a look in the bins tomorrow.'

'Can't we go out tonight?'

'If you insist,' said Perry. 'But this might be a lot easier in the morning.'

'We need to check, in case they've done the bins. Maybe they'll do them today. Maybe that's part of the plan.'

'No,' said Perry. 'Bin collections in the morning.'

'Then we'll go in the morning,' said Susan. 'I'm tired. It'll wait.'

'Okay,' said Perry. 'Let's call it a day and I'll see you in the morning. I'll phone the boss and tell her.'

Susan stood up and wandered over to don her denim jacket. Perry watched her. When she turned back, she smiled at him.

'I'll see you in the morning,' she said.

'Yes,' said Perry. She walked away, and he put his head down.

He gave half a smile. Tanya saying what she said, but possibly Susan also interested in him. Was she? Was she really?

'How did you know her again?' asked Susan, halting suddenly.

'Who?' said Perry.

'Tanya, who was in here. She's quite a good-looking woman, isn't she?'

'I hadn't noticed,' said Perry.

'Perry, you're a man,' said Susan. 'You noticed the moment Hope walked in. You noticed when I walked in. I want to bet that every man in here notices the shape and look of a woman that comes into the office.'

'Not every man,' said Perry. 'Not sure Ross does.'

'Stop it,' said Susan. 'You know what I'm saying.'

'What are you saying?'

'What was she talking to you about out there?' said Susan. 'She seems mighty keen on you.'

'She seems what?' said Perry.

'Mighty keen on you. The way she stood in front of you. That way she spoke to you. The way she adjusts her shoulders as she's talking. She almost, well . . .'

'What?'

'Like one of those birds, you know. Ruffle their feathers when they're attracting their mates.'

'Get out of it,' said Perry. 'You're being daft.'

'No,' said Susan. 'I'm a woman, I know what she's up to. You can tell. Don't blame her either,' said Susan.

Perry suddenly looked up and over at her, but she'd turned on her heel already. He watched as she walked out the door, the blonde hair swinging left and right, now wrapped back up in a ponytail because she was leaving.

'Susan,' he said, shouting after her, 'you know—'

'Trust me, I know,' said Susan. 'She's after you. Like I said, can't fault the woman for that, can you?' Susan gave a smile, which made Perry almost leap up off the seat. But he remained what he thought was cool, if that was still a thing these days, and let her leave.

For a moment, Perry stopped. Tanya was keen on him. If Susan hadn't been here, it wouldn't be a problem. They would just get to know each other again, get close, and see what happened. But a part of him wondered what Susan Cunningham now wanted.

Why me, why now? thought Perry. *Couldn't get a woman for ages, and like the buses, two of them come along at once. It's not fair. It's just not ruddy fair.*

Chapter 07

Hope had never been to Little Scatwell. She'd never heard of it, and as they approached, she realised why. It was small. A little hamlet, they might have said in England. A few houses. That being said, it wasn't an unattractive part of the world. You were surrounded by country here, on the other side of Lord Bairstow's estate. Away from it all.

Hope thought about her own place in Inverness. Maybe somewhere like this would be better for the wee one. You'd have a sizeable garden to run around in. Hope had never thought about a garden. She was happy in a flat, but it turned out John wanted a garden. Neither of them had planted a flower in their lives. But this, this was different. A child could play here.

Where was a child going to play in the flat? Did a new parent have time to maintain a garden? You would not let a couple-of-months-old baby roll around in the garden, would you? Or did you? Did you have to stimulate them early? Was it good for them to be out and hearing the birdsong? Hope shook herself. 'Focus,' she said. Ross turned the corner down a small lane and then stopped the car.

The headlights flooded the stonework at the front of a

cottage. Ross spotted the number painted on a piece of wood on the wall.

'This is it,' he said. He rolled the car further forward onto the drive before stopping. There was another car there. He made a note of the number plate.

'Looks like she's in,' said Hope. She checked her watch. It was late. Very late. Not a social time to call on someone. And there were no lights on within the cottage.

'Let's have a quick look around the outside,' said Hope. They approached the front door, but it was shut. She walked around, finding curtains drawn in every room she passed. The left-hand side of the house was just a wall. At the back, she found a locked door into a kitchen. Beyond was the garden, and a shed. Hope continued round and met Ross coming the other way. At this side of the house, they found a door, wide open. Hope could smell something coming from inside. It was like sewage. She choked back a cough.

Her stomach rolled. She didn't need this. She didn't need those sorts of smells, not with the way she felt normally.

'You okay?' asked Ross. He'd taken out a handkerchief and was placing it over his mouth and nose.

'I'll be fine,' she said. Hope took out a small pen torch and stepped inside the door, shining a light into the interior. There was a small hallway. When she pointed down to the floor, she could see what looked like muck. The door in front of her was open and led into a living room. When she stepped into it, however, she saw where the muck had come from.

In the middle of the living room was what looked like a small device, some sort of machine that could spray. It had an arm that seemed to rotate, and there was a tube running away from it back out past where they'd walked in. It was hard to see the tube in the torchlight.

Lights came on. Hope turned to see that Ross had flicked a switch.

'What on earth?' he said.

Hope tried not to breathe. She had to, of course. But she didn't want to breathe in through her nose because then she took the full smell full on. It was raw silage. She was sure of it. Muck spreading. It wasn't a large muck spreader, for they had got it in through the door. A small contraption. But it had done its work in this room. There was muck everywhere. But nobody was here.

'What on earth's this?' said Ross. 'I feel like I should go back out and put my wellies on.'

'We won't find anyone in, will we?' said Hope. 'This doesn't happen, and you leave the door open. You either leave or . . .'

'Or something more remiss has occurred.'

Hope looked around the room, for she'd also almost missed it in the spreading of the muck. The room had been tipped up here, there, and everywhere, stuff thrown around. She turned away and walked towards the kitchen, off another door from the living room. When she stepped in there, she saw again another place that was trashed, except this time there were lots of pictures sitting on a kitchen table.

She looked over at a couple of chairs that had been tipped over. There were ropes around them.

'Alan, look at this.'

Ross came through and knelt beside one of the chairs. 'Tied and then cut. There's plenty of blood around, too. Lots of it.' He then stood up and stared at the pictures on the kitchen table. 'Hope,' he said. 'These are, well, they're graphic.'

'I'd want to say they're erotic,' said Hope, looking at images

54

of a naked woman. 'But she doesn't really look happy in these, does she?' They were vulgar and very explicit.

Hope looked around the kitchen before entering another room. It was the bedroom and had been turned over, but there were pictures about and a woman appeared several times. She looked like a happier version of the woman in the kitchen table photos. Hope wondered if it was Lauren. She studied the face closely, got out her mobile phone and took a photograph of several of the pictures.

'Better call Jona out here,' she said over her shoulder as she heard Ross enter the room. 'We'll leave her to go through carefully. Something's obviously happened.'

She wondered exactly what had happened. The photographs—were they recent? When had they been done? She looked at the bed that had been overturned. There was nothing unusual on the sheets. She thought there was a sexual explanation to this. She was wondering if the bed had been used at all. Had somebody come and, well, made the woman endure something she really shouldn't have? It sent a chill through Hope.

Ross disappeared back out. He came back two minutes later. 'Bathroom's untouched,' he said. 'Can't find anyone in the house. It's just a one bedroom. Not that big a place.'

They walked back through to the kitchen and looked around again, not wanting to touch anything until Jona got there.

'Where is she then?' Hope asked Ross. 'Has she fled? Has she been taken?'

'Our man was tied up and dumped on the road,' said Ross. 'Maybe she's been taken too. If he's been playing around with her . . . maybe she had a boyfriend. Maybe—'

'Too many maybes,' said Hope. 'And where is she?'

Together, they stepped outside to look at the rest of the grounds of the cottage. They weren't large, a small garden at the rear. It was quite rough, a lawn that wasn't flat. The surface seemed to rise and fall here and there, as if it was a field that hadn't been properly prepped before the grass was grown on it. And there was a shed off to the side.

Hope wandered over to look at the shed. In the dark, it was hard to see, but her pen torch light ran round the door. There was a padlock on it, and she stepped back, wondering where the key might be. As she did so, her torch went to the ground, and she could see the discolouration. She bent down, her hand touching what looked like brown in the dark, but when she brought it up towards her nose, she could smell it was blood.

'See if we can find a key for this,' she said. She stepped up beside the shed and listened in, before saying, 'This is the police, is anyone in there? Can anybody hear me?'

It was silent. Having seen that she'd got no response, she heard Ross putting a phone call in to the station, requesting more backup, asking for Perry and Susan Cunningham.

'We've got ropes inside,' said Ross.

'What did Lord Bairstow say? She was missing today, nothing about being missing yesterday, just missing today. Did all this happen today, then?' she said. 'And the photographs, they're not, well . . .'

'They're not the sort of ones that are taken because she wanted them to be taken,' said Ross. 'I know some people get a big kick out of that. They love being on the camera, posing in front of it. Those aren't that type of thing. This looks like somebody today has come in and tied her up.'

'And tied somebody else up,' said Hope.

'Let's go back inside a minute,' she said. The pair re-entered

56

the kitchen, and Hope looked at the photographs again. Ross put on the main light of the kitchen, and Hope checked the photographs under it. She matched up the backgrounds. 'These are from today.'

Ross looked at them. 'They're on printer paper. Somebody's printed these off. Here.'

'Can you do that?'

'Yes, you can bring a printer. A portable one. Print them off. You can tell because the quality's not that good.'

'So someone's come in and tied her up along with somebody else. Made some explicit photographs as well. And then done what? Sprayed silage all over the front room.'

'Spurned lover,' said Ross. 'That's what it's saying, isn't it?'

'A spurned lover that had two mates in the back of a van and dumped the body. And was clever enough not to have that van appear on CCTV before it got there. Don't like this, Ross. I don't like it at all.'

Ross had taken out a latex glove for his hand and began opening the drawers.

'What are you doing?' asked Hope.

'See if I can find a key for the padlock out there. See if there's anything in that shed. You said there was a lot of blood in front of it.'

'Indeed,' said Hope.

Ross pulled open several drawers, and then he spotted it on the side of a cupboard. Sets of keys. He looked up and took several off.

'Only one of these will work,' he said. Hope followed him outside as he began to open up the lock. He tried several keys, but nothing worked until his penultimate one, where the lock turned easily. The padlock dropped slightly, freeing it, and Ross whipped it off. He pulled back the closure that the padlock kept in place, and then went to open the door.

'Careful,' said Hope. 'Don't want to disturb anything inside.'

Ross pulled the door back and stepped away from it. The interior was pitch black, and Hope pointed her pen torch down initially, following the trail of blood that led onto a wooden floor. On the floor was a set of clothes. They looked like women's clothes, possibly a skirt, a blouse, something she would wear to work.

'That's not good,' said Hope.

'I'm not quite sure which part of all of this is good,' said Ross. 'The silage, the blood and everything overturned, explicit photographs, tied up, and now blood out here.'

Hope ran her torch up, but the shed had what looked like a wheelbarrow stuck on the front with some wood beside it. Hope couldn't really see in properly. She scanned the floor again with her torch. 'I think I can get round there, Alan. Avoid that blood.'

'You'll have to glove up. Do you want me to do it?'

'No,' said Hope, half because, as the lead investigator, she wanted to be first there. And half just to prove that this pregnant woman was still a detective. She reached into her pocket and pulled out some gloves. Once she had them on, she stepped forward, put her hands on the edge of the door, and swung herself round past the blood inside the shed.

Hope pulled her torch out from between her teeth and shone it across the floor. It highlighted the blood spatter here, there, and everywhere. The torch beam ascended the wall in front of her. There was a bench from side to side in the shed, an anvil on the top, but underneath were flowerpots.

She scanned the left-hand side of the rear wall and could

see some basic tools, and saws. There was a spade hanging, and as she drifted across, she saw some smaller shelves higher up. A plant pot. There was a car battery, of all things. Then there were some of those solar lights. The pen torch ran across into the darkest recesses, and then Hope stumbled backwards, hitting the edge of the shed.

There was a face looking back at her. The torchlight dropped away quickly. Hope took a deep breath. She put her torch up again, illuminating a face with the blood drained from it, eyes staring out towards her. There was no body attached. It was Lauren. At least it was the woman in the photographs in the house.

Hope felt the rush. She felt the drive from her stomach, the twist in it, and it took everything she had to not step in the blood as she swung herself back outside.

'You okay?' asked Ross. Hope ignored him, disappearing off to a flower bed and retching violently above it.

Chapter 08

'Quite the scene,' said Perry. He was driving with Susan back from Little Scatwell, where the pair of them had spent most of the night. It was now early morning, and Hope, having been quite taken by Susan's idea about the van, had directed them to follow it up. The scene at Little Scatwell was now in the hands of Jona Nakamura and her team, and Hope thought one of the best opportunities for progress was to trace the van. It had to be the same person who killed Lauren and Kevin, after all, didn't it? It made sense. At least it was a good line of inquiry.

'I'm shattered,' said Susan from the passenger seat.

'Wasn't a good sight, was it? The boss looked quite, well, jaded. Can't be easy when you're pregnant.'

'I don't think it'd be easy for anybody seeing that head straight off. Not used to seeing a detached face.'

'No,' said Perry. 'It was brutal. And those photographs. Pretty sick.'

'Not sure it's that normal, either. If you've been jilted or you've been made a fool of in love because she's off with another man, to actually make her expose herself like that and take photographs? And do what with them? Photographs to embarrass her by putting them elsewhere, maybe, but she's dead,' said Susan. 'I'm not quite with that. I don't follow the logic.'

'Well, sometimes there isn't a logic,' said Perry. 'We've got to focus on our van, anyway. So where do we start?'

Perry had driven back over the bridge into Inverness, and was now turning back at the roundabout to go back over the bridge.

'It was seen coming over the bridge with all its cameras. Another traffic one, just a little up from that, too. So, we start from there.'

'So where was the last one?'

'Just before North Kessock turnoff.'

'So where would they dump this decal?' asked Perry. 'You're not going to run up somebody's drive and throw stuff in their bin, are you?'

'No, but we can check all the other public bins.'

Perry turned off into North Kessock. It was just beyond the Kessock Bridge, close to the water's edge. Dawn was in full flow, the hour being just after seven. Perry stopped, allowing Susan to get out and delve her hands into the public bins.

He watched her dismantle them and pull out the bags, looking inside before reassembling the bin. When she got back in, she'd drawn a brief sketch that was used to mark off each bin that they'd gone to. They found some larger bins in a car parking area and checked those as well.

And then they drove along, looking to see if there were any bins from houses that sat close to the road. They found a few where the bins were located inside little pens, close to the pavement. Susan knocked on the door of the house, asking to check the bin before continuing her mission. It took them the best part of three hours to complete North Kessock. At which point, Susan looked fed up.

'It was a good idea,' said Perry.

'Check the bins further up. There must be some on the way up to the site where they dumped the body,' said Susan.

Perry drove on up the A9, past the Munlochy turnoff, before arriving at a layby just before the spot where the body had been dumped. There was a bin there that Susan checked, but again came up empty. She was looking for a blue type of cellophane that would be on the side of the van. But there was nothing. All morning, there had been nothing.

'Of course, they may have just come back in a car and taken it out again,' said Perry.

'Really?' said Susan. 'You would risk that?'

'Well, probably not,' said Perry. 'If, and I mean if, they've got some kind of decal across the van, and have whipped it off, they're probably going to dump it and go. They won't want any attention, will they? They're not thinking that we've spotted this and is what we're looking for.'

'Well, it's not here,' said Susan.

Perry drove down to the roundabout at Tore, spun round, and came back. There was a little pastry shop at North Kessock right beside where everyone watched the dolphin viewpoint. He had to cross the bridge again to come back to get to it, but he was ready for something to eat. He left Susan in the car while he picked up a couple of coffees and came back with some croissants.

'Get that down you. It's been a long night,' said Perry.

'Maybe they didn't dump it here,' said Susan. 'Maybe they dumped it somewhere else.'

'Where else are you going to dump it?' said Perry. 'We've come up here. North Kessock's on the left-hand side. We've searched North Kessock. There's the lay-by further up. We've checked that as well. We drove up the hard shoulders. Not seeing anything dumped out there. Maybe they took it away with them. Not sure they would do that, but it's quite a lot of decal to cover a van like that. It's going to be big and get in the way. You've got a body in the back already. You've then got to dump it afterwards, handle it again. It's a thought,' said Perry. 'All I'm saying is your idea might be correct.'

Susan was sitting and looking out from the car towards the water just beside North Kessock.

'So you knew Tanya from Glasgow,' said Susan.

'Yes, I knew Tanya in Glasgow. Why? Why do you keep asking about her?'

'Just wondering about her. So, when you recommended her to Macleod, that was because of what?'

'When I went down to investigate in Glasgow, Tanya was the only one who spoke to me at the station. I thought she was happily married and elsewhere, and then I found out she wasn't, and she said to me she always thought up further north was nice. I put a word in for her with Macleod. We needed someone we could trust. I know I can trust her.'

'Were you close?' asked Susan.

'We were good friends.'

'Really good friends?' asked Susan.

'We were friends,' said Perry. 'We had to trust each other, like you and I trust each other.'

'I thought you said she worked in HR.'

'She did,' said Perry.

'That's not the same as us trusting each other, is it? I mean, you and I, we've been out on cases. You've got people running around who could do harm to you. You don't really trust HR in the same way. I mean, visiting HR isn't really a risk.'

'Look, I just knew her. I gave her a hand up here, okay?'

Susan tucked into a croissant, and the subject dropped. 'There's a roundabout there at North Kessock, isn't there?'

'Yes,' said Perry. 'You turn off.'

'It goes under the road, onto the Black Isle.'

'Yes,' said Perry. 'The Drumsmittal Road. I think that's what they call it.'

'You could go up there. There will not be cameras up there, will there? There are no cameras up the Drumsmittal Road.'

'Well, it's kind of a back way onto the Black Isle, so I guess probably not.'

'Eat up,' said Susan. 'We need to check up there.'

Perry sighed and shoved his croissant down his throat. He washed it down quickly, started the engine and drove off. Susan obviously had a bee in her bonnet about this and although he didn't want to tell her, she was probably wrong. He didn't really want to be driving halfway across the Black Isle checking bins, either. It was an idea, a decent idea, but it wasn't really working.

Perry turned off at North Kessock, found the small roundabout, and then routed back underneath the A9 and out on the Drumsmittal Road. It went up through trees, and eventually, houses appeared at the side. They were set back off the road, and as they rounded a bend, they could see a bin lorry up ahead.

'No,' said Susan. 'No, no, it's not collection day, it can't be. Get up, get up to that lorry.'

Perry almost sighed, but he drove up to park behind the bin lorry. Two bin attendants were bringing out bins to load them up onto the rear of the lorry for emptying. Susan stepped out of the car, warrant card in hand.

'Excuse me, gentlemen, I'm Detective Constable Susan Cunningham. Can you just stop?'

The two bin men looked at her. One was a large man, and his bright fluorescent jacket made him look like a giant beacon. The other was slimmer, slightly shorter, and looked at her warily.

'Sorry, can we help?' he said.

'How many of the houses here have you done?'

'Well, those ones,' said the man, pointing back down the road. Susan counted.

'So, ten of them?'

'Yes, about ten of them,' he said.

'Did you notice in any of the bins, if there was a blue cellophane-type wrap, lots of it?'

'Gotta be honest with you, love,' said the big man. 'We don't have a peek inside all the bins. You wheel them onto the back, and you dump it. I mean, we might have seen it if it was on top, but if it was not on top, probably not, and even then, who knows?'

'Can I see inside the lorry?'

'You what?' said the man. 'What do you mean inside?'

'I want to see inside the lorry. All the rubbish.'

'Hang on a minute,' said the man. He walked round to the side of the lorry, banged on the door. The driver came out and walked round to the back.

'John here says you want to look in the back of the lorry.'

'Yes,' said Susan. Perry had joined her now. 'I'm afraid we need to look in the back of the lorry.'

'I can take it back to the dump site. Empty it there. You can have a look.'

'I take it, it all mashes up inside,' said Susan.

'Yes. The more you put in it, obviously it has to compact it, otherwise these lorries would be full,' said the man.

'Can I get to look inside it now?'

'Okay,' said the man.

Behind him, Perry could see a couple of cars had now slowed down. The bin lorry was blocking the road to a large degree. But the fact it was stopped and they were around it had blocked the road completely. Both directions were blocked.

'Maybe we can move somewhere else,' said Perry.

'Where would you like me to go?' said the driver. 'It's like this the whole way up. It's difficult to just pull off into somewhere. Not with something this size on this type of road.'

'I'm only just going to get up into it, okay?' said Susan.

'Is that thing isolated?' asked Perry.

'You don't think I'm going to let her go anywhere near it if it's not isolated,' said the driver. 'I've isolated everything; it won't work. I'm not sure how much she's going to see, but you can climb up there, love, if you really want to. Personally, I wouldn't advise it. I mean, I'm not suggesting you don't take a look. But I am suggesting we go back to the depot and you go there to have a look if you really need to get inside this lorry. I mean, it's not a body or anything, is it?'

'Hopefully not,' said Susan. She jumped up onto the stand where the bins were normally put and then clambered up to look inside the rear of the lorry. It was divided in two and she looked inside the first one.

'That's the recycled stuff,' said the man. Susan pulled her head back out.

'Get the big torch from the car, Perry,' she said. Perry did so and noticed the drivers looking at him. He held up his warrant card, showing it was police, and put up an appreciative hand, asking for a bit of patience.

He returned to the bin lorry with the torch from the boot of the car and handed it to Susan. She spent the next two minutes shining it around inside the recycled section of the bin lorry.

'Nothing in there,' she said. Susan swung round and looked inside the other one.

'Perry,' she said.

'What?' he said.

'Glove. Give me a glove. Has anybody got one of those like grabbers?'

'A what?' said the driver.

'Have you got a grabber? One of those long things with a grabber at the end. I can see something, but I don't want to put my foot in properly. I'm not sure what's going to drop.'

'I said we can take it down to the depot and dump it there,' said the driver. 'You can have a proper look through it.'

'We're not going to stop you doing your rounds if it's unnecessary,' said Susan.

One of the other bin men disappeared into the lorry and came back with a grabber. He handed it to Susan, and she reached in, torch in one hand, and nearly fell over.

'Perry, support me,' she said. Perry stood behind her, his hands up on her hips, Susan's backside inches from his face. His proximity to her and his handling of her hips made Perry a little awkward. He could see the looks of the two bin men, but he ignored them.

'Got something,' said Susan. She seemed to pull at first with the grabber and then reached in with her hand. 'Help me down,' she said to Perry. He wrapped his arms around her waist and lifted her backwards before setting her on the ground. As he did so, Susan pulled out a long stream of blue cellophane-type material.

'I'm going to have to ask you gentlemen to stop your business right now. I need to get someone here from our forensic department. This is what we're looking for,' she said. She turned to Perry. 'I'll give Jona a call. Get her over here.'

'I guess I'll try to work out something to do with this traffic,' said Perry. 'Well done, though. Boss will be happy.'

Perry began moving the traffic while Susan made a phone call. She came back a couple of minutes later and sat watching Perry waving the traffic this way and that.

'We make a good team, don't we?' she said. 'When we work closely together?'

'You did well. I'm not sure I would have followed that idea through as thoroughly as that.'

'You still came with me,' said Susan. Behind them, one of the bin men came over.

'You got what you wanted. Once they come and remove it, can we get back to our business?'

'Yes, you can. I'm sorry about that, but I had to trace this.'

'Well, well done,' said the binman. 'You're not just a pretty face, then.'

Perry thought he heard Susan, as she turned to walk away, say, 'No, not like Tanya.'

Chapter 09

Seoras Macleod pulled up in his car near the small cottage in Little Scatwell. He couldn't get down the driveway because of the number of police cars around it, but he saw the forensic wagon parked in close. He scanned the scene and then saw the red hair and ponytail of the person he was looking for.

Hope had pale skin, but today she looked positively white. They'd found the body, or at least the head, close to midnight. Macleod had been alerted around five in the morning. That was fine. It was a case. He wasn't the lead investigator. So, it was okay not to tell him things, if they weren't time critical. But having been told, he decided he wanted to come out and see for himself what was going on.

'Rough one then,' said Macleod, approaching Hope.

'Oh, good morning. Yes, you could say that.'

'How are you doing?'

'Well, I'm still here and I'm still going. I could do with my bed and some good food.'

'How much longer do you need to be here?' asked Macleod.

'Probably not that much longer. Why?'

'I'll take you and Ross for breakfast, if you want. I take it he's still about, and the rest of the team.'

'Perry and Susan off looking for van decals in the bins around North Kessock.'

'What?' said Macleod.

'Susan's got this idea that the van came in disguise, with decals on it. Says she's seen a van, exactly the same size, same type of tyres arriving. Believes they must have dumped the decals somewhere.'

'You reckon that's a goer?' asked Macleod.

'It's worth a punt. We're not getting anywhere else with the van. They were out here last night with me, but I told them to get that done this morning.'

'And Ross is still here, is he?'

'Ross is being Ross. Organising for me.'

'You up for taking me on a tour?' asked Macleod.

'Why are you out here?' asked Hope. 'You're more than welcome, but why are you out here?'

'Fancied a look,' said Macleod.

'What do you mean by you fancied a look?'

'Well, it's a decapitated head, and a body dumped on the road. We've seen quite a few murders. But this is . . . well, it's brutal, but it's set up as a domestic, or at least, not family domestic, but a lovers' domestic. Somebody from the past. What about boyfriends? What do we know?'

'I'm going to head back over to Lord Bairstow's and see who Lauren Starr's friends were. Check if anybody out there knows, but they talked about her having an affair with MacTavish. That would make it about MacTavish's partner. Seemed quite a jump. She was over most of the day anyway with Emma MacTavish. Anne Lewis doesn't seem the type to me.'

'Woman scorned though.'

'Oh yes, speaking of which,' said Hope, 'Perry and Susan.'

'What about them?' asked Macleod.

'Didn't quite seem themselves. Perry seemed very defensive around her. They were really chatty. She was probing him for something.'

'I think Perry may be the victim of desire,' said Macleod.

'What the hell's that meant to mean?' asked Hope.

'You ever thought Perry wanted a woman?'

'Well, he was very keen on Susan for a while, but she wasn't so much on him.'

'No, but there's another woman in town now who is, I think, very keen on Perry. And I think Susan may have reappraised her position.'

'Oh.'

'And that,' said Macleod, 'is as far as I'm going. I do not get involved in personal relationships. If it becomes an issue—'

'What, you're going to speak to them?'

'No, if it becomes an issue, you'll speak to them,' said Macleod. 'Like I said, I don't get involved.'

'Better suit up,' said Hope. 'Not sure Jona is finished with everything. She gets very particular about her crime scenes.'

'She'll be fine with me,' said Macleod, but he headed over to the forensic wagon, anyway. Five minutes later, he joined Hope, having changed, and walked in through the front door of the cottage.

'Silage,' said Macleod. 'A silage machine as well. Well, a small one.'

'It's from down the road. It's been stolen,' said Hope. 'But somebody obviously knew how to use it.'

'Where did the silage come from, though?'

'It's a couple of oil drums, well, drums of silage outside. You don't need that much to spray a room.'

'No, but you have to bring it here,' said Macleod. 'It has to come in the back of something.'

'These ones you could have got in the back of a decent sized car. We've canvassed around, but nobody saw anything. It's kind of hidden away, this house.'

'It is, isn't it?' said Macleod. 'If you knew where it was, you would know it would be a good place to carry this out.'

'Exactly,' said Hope.

Macleod continued to tour, noting how everything had been overturned.

'What's the point of tipping it all up?' said Macleod. 'I don't get this. We then have provocative photographs, I'm told.'

'They're not provocative. More abusive. She was clearly made to strip down and pose in, well, it was no fashion shoot. Very explicit. You can see on her face she's traumatised.'

Macleod entered the kitchen with Hope. He saw the photographs, his face contorting at them.

'Over there,' said Hope, 'is where they were tied up at one point.'

'They?'

'Two sets of ties. Two chairs. Somebody else was here.'

'You find any DNA?'

'Bit early for that.'

'If MacTavish was brought here, DNA would be here on that seat.'

'If he was having an affair, his DNA would be here anyway,' said Hope. 'Not going to prove anything, is it?'

Macleod wandered into the other rooms of the house.

'There are not many photographs, are there? I can see Lauren,' he said. 'There's no other man in the house, though, except for that one. But there's none of him with Lauren, really.'

'Oh, yes, there is,' said Hope. She pointed down to a couple on the floor. 'But they're not embracing, they're not, well, anything. They're sort of stood side by side.'

'What do you think?' asked Macleod.

'That looks like a sibling. Possibly a brother. I got Ross to get on to it. See if he can find out if she's got any.'

'Very good,' said Macleod. He walked out with Hope to the shed. She stood outside while he went in. When he came back out, his face was in a grimace.

'That's not something you want to see every day,' he said.

'No, it isn't, Seoras,' said Hope.

'I don't understand this,' he said.

'What do you not understand?' asked Hope.

'I don't get why his body is taken and dumped. Why would you dump him out on the road?'

'Well, maybe she wanted to humiliate him. Or whoever wanted to, you know.'

'Humiliate him? He's dead,' said Macleod. 'It doesn't work. It doesn't make sense. This whole thing makes no sense. She's had her head cut off and put in the shed. Why?'

'It might be from rage,' said Hope.

'Rage?' said Macleod. 'And if the rage is to cut her head off and put it in the shed, why not do the same to him? Why is the place a mess and he's been wrapped up in the chair, and yet he's dumped on the road? This doesn't work,' said Macleod. 'It really doesn't work.'

'We need to find out who that man is in the photographs, though.'

'Yes, you do,' said Macleod, 'but he's nobody. Well, he's nobody in regards to this.'

73

'You so sure?'

'Why? Who do you think he is?'

'Well, he's standing aloof, so you could think that's a sibling, but maybe it's someone she knows who wants to be closer than she wants him to be. Maybe he then gets jealous that she's seeing MacTavish.'

'It's overkill,' said Macleod. 'If you want somebody to believe that this is rage, if you want somebody to believe that this is some sort of love triangle, then you're having to sell that rage. But they've oversold it. Really oversold it. This is somebody who doesn't see rage that often.

'Also, three people in the van dumping his body. Three men. Where do they come from? What have they got to do with this? You just pitch up with a gaggle of brothers to help you out? People don't do that. People don't come along and participate in decapitation. Decapitation? It's not right. That happens from somebody being wild. Or somebody trying to show it to be wild. Why in the shed? Why not just leave them at the scene? This whole thing makes no sense to me,' said Macleod.

Ross appeared, marching towards them both. 'Morning, sir,' he said, and then turned to Hope. 'The man in the photographs is Lauren's brother,' said Ross. 'He lives in New Zealand, has done for years. Photographs are obviously from when they met.'

'See?' Macleod said. 'Don't like this.'

'So, it's a set-up then,' said Hope. 'If we treat this as a set-up, a set-up for what? Why? Why would you kill MacTavish and then kill Lauren Starr? Why would you set them up as a couple?'

'What have we been sold?' asked Macleod.

'Well,' said Hope. 'We've been told by this action that there was an affair going on between MacTavish and Lauren Starr. MacTavish's body is then dumped. She's killed. We're being told that there's a third party who is angry at their affair.'

'Do we know there's definitely an affair? Are we sure that they're sleeping together? Do we know that there's anything going on between them?'

'She's not reported in to work,' said Hope. 'He didn't come in to work that day either. Said he was off to get a package. A package that the company said they knew nothing about.'

'So,' said Macleod, 'off to get a package the company knew nothing about. Do we know for sure it's him that rang in? Do we know—?'

'Whoa,' said Hope. 'He didn't ring in. The company, when he didn't come, rang in looking for him.'

'And,' said Macleod, 'the reason we think he's gone off to get the package is what?'

'That's what he told his partner.'

'But,' said Macleod, 'we don't know what he was doing. We don't know if that ended up as a problem.'

'Well, it was a lie because there was no package to get for the company.'

'What about Lauren?' asked Macleod.

'Well, she's just not checked in. She phoned in sick.'

'Really?' said Macleod. 'We're going to have to look closely at where our information's coming from. We're being sold a story, Hope. If we're being told a tale, it's being woven for a reason. And we can't just accept everything. We're going to have to question everything we know. And we're going to have to question where it came from to unravel this one.'

'I just don't get where a single killer comes into this,' said Hope. 'Why is he killing Lauren Starr? Why is he dumping

MacTavish's body for attention on the A9? It doesn't make sense. Why go to the bother of getting a silage sprayer and plastering the inside of the house? Why is he making her do provocative photographs before killing her? It's just—'

'It's not right,' said Macleod. 'And we just don't see it at the moment. That's the problem. We're not seeing it from where it's coming from. What the real purpose is behind it. But you will. Anyway, you're probably starving. Let's go get you and Ross some breakfast.'

Chapter 10

'Bloody hell, Jenny, come on!'

Jane Farrow was not happy. It was meant to be a good night out. She was nineteen and currently waiting to get home. The plan had been that Jane would drive Jenny and Kim down to the party in the nightclub and then back again. Jane wasn't going to drink.

Her father told her not to drink and as it was his car, it was best that she didn't. But then again, she didn't realise at the time that she was going to meet Andy. She'd had her eyes on Andy for a while. He was very cool. He was very swish and she was just glad that night she had worn something a little more exciting than what she'd planned.

Andy wasn't meant to be at this party. And in fact, he hadn't been. He'd wandered in with a few of his mates, into a private do. Jane, until that point, hadn't had anything to drink. Not until Andy came over to her.

He had offered to get her a drink. She'd started off with just the one. That was all right. A glass of wine at that time of night. She'd have been good to drive. But then she'd gone on to the shots as well. Well, she was having fun with him and they'd made out right there in the bar. She'd got his phone number as well. He'd said he was going to call her. They could go out maybe tomorrow.

She'd got excited, carried away. She'd then bought more drinks, and she quickly found out that she'd run out of money. Jenny and Kim had also had a good night. Jane was going to drive them home about two in the morning.

But she'd had to wait now while Jenny was in a back alley with some guy she'd met. Thankfully, Andy hadn't suggested that. Yes, they'd made out, but she would have a bit more class about her than Jenny. She would not let some boy have her in the back alley.

Kim was running lookout and Jane was walking around in a stomp now. She'd been in her high heels for too long. Her legs were cold because of the short skirt. And as for her top, well, she'd worn that one that certainly grabbed Andy's attention. Trouble was that without a jacket at this time of night, it was like the worst blanket you could ever imagine.

She'd also had drinks, so she was cold from that. She had the keys for the car with her and she'd brought some cash, but hadn't her purse with her cards. The buses had gone, and so the only option now was to drive home. She wasn't going to call her dad and get him to come down and pick her up in her mum's car. No way. She'd get the car back. After all, she was okay. Yes, she'd had a lot to drink, but she could focus, unlike Jenny and Kim.

'Come on,' said Jane. 'Is he not done by now?'

'You're not usually complaining if boys last long,' said Kim, laughing. Jane wasn't waiting for this. She turned and stomped back in her high heels, round and round, getting more and more annoyed. She looked across and saw some people moseying about. There was a kebab van further down. She'd get something from there, but she'd no money. She just wanted to go home.

A couple of minutes later, she saw Jenny adjusting her skirt and walking back over towards where Kim was on lookout.

'Well, girls,' she said, 'that was worth it.'

Kim burst out laughing. Jane just shook her head at Jenny. 'We need to get home. It's bloody freezing. What the hell were you doing, anyway?'

'What wasn't he doing?'

Jane had enough of this. 'Car now, come on!'

Together, they stumbled around and eventually made it to the street where Jane had left the car. If you were clever, you could find the right place to leave the car. In Inverness, it was difficult to not be in a paying place, even at night. But Jane knew her city. And yes, it was a short walk, but it was a walk she was capable of. Albeit, she had to keep shouting for Jenny and Kim to keep up.

The biggest problem was that the three of them lived in Elgin, but that wasn't where she was going for a night out. For a proper night out, they went to Inverness. Jane was at the college in Inverness, but she lived at home, unlike Andy, who she'd seen about the college during the day. But now she had to get home, which was a reasonable drive out to Elgin. She started the car up, and beside her, Kim let out a massive burp.

'Hey, hey,' said Kim. 'Better out than in.' She reached down into her handbag and pulled out a bottle of vodka. 'You want some?' said Kim to Jane.

'I'm driving,' said Jane.

'You're pissed up anyway.'

'And I've got to drive home. So no, just be on the lookout, okay? In case the cops are about.'

Jane started the car. Yes, she was okay. She was good. Jane

put the car into gear, then realised that she'd not put the clutch in enough, and the car stalled. The other two laughed.

'Shut up,' said Jane, 'this is serious; otherwise, we're sleeping in here tonight.'

'I don't care,' said Jenny, 'I'm in heaven.'

'Shut her up,' said Jane to Kim, but Kim was just laughing. Jane started the car again, and this time, she was able to get it going.

'Drive at thirty,' Kim said. 'Don't let them know you're drunk.'

The car made its way out onto the main road out towards the airport, and then further towards Elgin. When she was driving out of the city, Jane was okay, because there were plenty of streetlights on. But once she cleared the city, she got on to long, albeit dual, carriageways, but ones that were not lit. Jane also didn't have her glasses with her. She didn't think that Andy liked her glasses. Some boys did. She was sure of it. She'd been told she was cute in them, but not by Andy. So, she hadn't worn them in case she met him. That meant that her long vision wasn't quite what it should be. In the early evening, driving without glasses was easy. Not in this darkness.

Jane peered forward, shouting that the other girls should watch for any other cars on the road. They yelled that one was behind them, and it tore off past them. Jane looked down at the speedometer.

She was doing thirty. You could go up to sixty on this dual carriageway. She pulled over for a minute, onto the hard shoulder, switched off all the lights, and took a deep breath. *Get yourself together*, she thought.

'Why are we stopped? Why are we stopped?' shouted Jenny from the back seat.

'Shut the hell up,' said Jane. Jane loved her friends, except right now she didn't.

She went to start the car, but the passenger door opened, and Kim stepped out. Jane could hear the vomiting and the spitting. And then Kim got back in.

'That's better. Let's go, James, John, driver, whatever you're called.'

Jane started the car again and pulled out onto the road. About ten seconds later, she remembered to switch the lights on. This time, she looked at the speedometer. Fifty. Fifty was good. Fifty was a car that was being sensible. You couldn't get pulled over for doing fifty. If you were doing thirty, you would look stupid.

No, fifty was good. Jane kept the driving going. And then she realised she was in one lane, and then the other, and then another. No, hang on. There were only two lanes. She could only be in two lanes. She must be going between both lanes.

There was an almighty bang.

The car seemed to jump, almost. Then it lurched to one side. And then it spun before stopping.

'Shit,' said Jane.

'Aw-oh,' said Kim. Jane wanted to tell her to shut the hell up, but Kim was already climbing out of the car.

'What the hell was that?' said Jenny from the back seat. Jane opened her car door and in her high heels tottered round to the rear. The road behind them was dark. Their car had spun and ended up sideways across the road. The rear lights provided light only across the road, not back down it from where they'd come. The headlights, similarly, were shining across and showed the central reservation.

'You need your thingies on,' said Kim.

'What?'

'You need the thingies on. We're stopped on the road. You need the thingies on.'

It took Jane a moment before she realised Kim meant the hazard lights.

'Jenny, switch the hazard lights on.'

'Where's the thing for that?'

Jenny doesn't drive, Jenny doesn't bloody drive, thought Jane, and she tottered back to the car. The button, like in most cars, was in the middle of the central dashboard. And she pressed it.

'Yay!' shouted Kim from down the road. 'Look at those flash!'

Jane began to stomp down the road behind the car towards Kim.

'What the hell did I hit?' she said.

'Don't know,' said Kim.

Kim stumbled on while Jane turned to look at the car. There was a large dent in the rear bumper. The car also seemed to be dented in the middle somewhere. *Bollocks*, thought Jane, *Dad's going to be raging*. She heard Kim cry out.

Kim had hit the ground hard, but Jane couldn't see her. 'You okay?'

'Ah, my bloody knee. Shitting hell.'

Somewhere Kim was rolling around on the ground and Jane tottered back to the car. She opened the boot, looked down and pulled up the carpet on the floor of the boot. Underneath it would be the jack, but also a torch that her father kept there. *He's almost anal*, she thought, *keeping all these things for breakdowns*.

She grabbed the torch, switched it on at the second attempt, and on tippy toes, walked back down the road to find Kim. The torch swept this way and that, until it came across a figure on the road. She stepped carefully over to it.

'Kim,' she said, and bent down to grab her friend. Except this person was tied, and the torch's beam flashed around the mid-rift of the person. She thought, *Kim doesn't have one of those*. And then Jane fell backwards, scrabbling away.

'Kim, there's a, there's a—'

'A what?' yelled Kim.

Jane could hear Kim working her way back towards her. And then Kim let out a scream.

'What the hell's that? What the f—?'

A car door behind her was opened, and Jenny could be heard tottering along. Jane, however, shone her torch towards what she had stumbled upon. There was a man's body there. The torch shook, as Jane could not control herself. But that was a man. From behind her, she heard Jenny's shriek.

'You've bloody killed him!'

'He's tied up,' said Jane. 'How did I kill him? He's tied up. Why is a nude man in the road, tied up?'

'Oh, crapping hell,' said Kim.

Jane swung the torch up, trying to find Kim, and saw her standing up a few feet behind the body. Kim put her hands up, waving them around, tottering towards Jane, but she was also walking towards the body. She fell over it.

'There are lights coming,' cried Jenny. 'There's a light. Bloody hell, it's police. That must be police, is it?'

A car was coming, white lights shining in the dark. Jane thought it was hammering along so quick. And then she heard it brake violently. It stopped only three or four feet from the man's body on the road. Blue lights illuminated on top of the car and some people got out. Torches were switched on.

'Bloody hell! Jones, call it in! Call it in!'

'Neil,' said the other one. And then they were talking into the radio. A face appeared beside Jane.

'Are you okay, ma'am? What happened? What—'

Lights passed over the man's body. 'Bloody hell. He looks dead. He looks dead!'

'That's not good,' said Jenny suddenly. And then she collapsed on the road. Jane's eyes filled with tears. And she shook as she cried.

Chapter 11

'Crap! It's not even 4 a.m.,' said Hope.

'Easy. Easy,' said John. Hope switched on the light beside the bed, and suddenly felt John reach for her. 'I've got to go. I've got another one,' she said.

'Easy on it, yes? If he's dead, you won't have to rush.'

A pair of arms pulled her in close, and a hand slid down onto her belly. 'Look after that one.'

She felt a kiss on her shoulder as she rolled out of bed. Hope reached over, pulled out a pair of pants and her pregnancy jeans, pulling them on before looking for the rest of her underwear and a black t-shirt. Soon she was wrapped up in a leather jacket as well, with her hair tied in a ponytail. She looked back towards the bed where John was lying half asleep.

'You're an inspiration when I see you like that,' she said. 'Just so vibrant and awake.'

He scrunched his eyes up. 'Is that a vision I see before me?'

'Shut up,' she said. 'I'm not coming back to bed. I've got a job to do.'

'If you can meet for breakfast, I'll buy you some,' he said.

'It's a dead body,' said Hope, going out of the bedroom door. 'You'll be lucky to see me today.' She made her way into the kitchen, grabbed a croissant from out of the cupboard, and

85

then made herself a quick cup of instant coffee.

She had five minutes to throw it down her throat, before there was a beep from the parking area below her flat. Hope rushed down and joined Susan Cunningham in her car.

'Out on the road towards Elgin, near the airport,' said Susan. 'Dumped in the road by the looks of it again.'

'Who found it this time?' said Hope.

'Well, apparently a car ran over him.'

'What?' said Hope.

'Yes, somebody drove into the body. I'm sure we'll see when we get there.'

'Anything else new since I went to bed?' asked Hope.

'We got all of that blue cellophane material out, and it is for a large vehicle decal, but one you can pull off. I sent it away with Jona to get examined, see if we can find anything more out about it.'

'That was a good grab,' said Hope. 'Really good one. What else?'

'Not to do with our case, but another kid got taken.'

'What?' said Hope.

'Another kid got taken out of a pram.'

'I wouldn't have thought I'd see that sort of thing round Inverness,' said Hope. 'Crazy.'

'No, but uniforms have been run ragged again.'

Susan continued to drive until they came to a police cordon. Diversions had been set up for normal cars to go round the section of road that was now closed off. But Hope and Susan were directed on through the cordon and up towards where an extensive set of lights lit up the road. Hope saw Jona Nakamura on scene, organising her people, and she told Susan to park over near where the forensic wagon was.

'Good morning,' said Hope. 'You're raising me from my bed again.'

'Bed?' said Jona. 'You got to bed? How did you get to bed? I haven't stopped. Between you lot and uniform, we're on the go 24-7.'

'You getting anywhere with the missing kids?'

'How do I know? I just look over what's there. I tell you what I find; you guys get on with it. And then I get shunted off to the next thing.'

Jona was in a coverall suit and handed Hope another. 'I found some ID on the body,' said Jona. 'It says Sean Devereaux,' she said.

Hope took a photograph of the ID inside the plastic evidence bag and then looked over her shoulder. She heard a car pulling up. Ross and Perry got out and approached her.

'Okay, morning, gentlemen,' said Hope. 'I'm going to take a look at the body with Jona. Ross, see who the witnesses are, who ran him over. Perry, here's an ID for you—Sean Devereaux—see if you can find me an address.'

'What about me?' asked Susan.

'Go to uniform, see what else they've found out. Check for CCTV as well, in the area. Might have been nighttime, but we want to know if this body came from a van as well. See what witnesses we've got.'

Susan nodded. Hope watched her team disperse while she got into the coverall suit.

'Still got the issues with the little one?' asked Jona. 'You getting your rest?'

Hope raised her eyebrows. 'Rest? When do I get rest from stuff like this?'

'You need to get your rest,' said Jona seriously.

'No, no, no,' said Hope. 'You're not doing that. I have enough people telling me to get my rest. I'll take it from John. Seoras has been told where he can hang that hat. And the team. You don't get to do that.'

'If you don't want the wisdom I've built up over my years, that's your business. But you are tired. You need to get the rest. Don't be afraid to take some time off. Dump it on Seoras.'

'I'm on top of this,' said Hope. 'All right, I'm on top of it.'

'It's not like last time,' said Jona. 'That time you jumped off the boat and the boat exploded behind you. Not like that. You're further on. You've got to be careful.'

'Stop lecturing,' said Hope, zipping up her coverall.

'Then start taking care of yourself,' said Jona. 'You'll get no second chances with that little one in there.'

'I do realise that!' But inside, she was a detective and there was a case on the go. She couldn't walk away.

Hope walked out into the middle of the road and saw the body lying there. The man was naked. He was maybe in his fifties or sixties and he had been tied up. His body had been hit hard by the car, from what Hope could see.

'You said you had ID. He's naked again.'

'Yes,' said Jona. 'Bit of a surprise when you pull some ID out of his hand.'

'It hadn't fallen out?'

'Tucked into a hand that's set tight with rigor mortis. Hands were also tied, tied tight together. Probably one of the most protected areas. They made sure we got the ID.'

'And that car there?' said Hope.

'That's the one that ran him over. The three girls, I'm not sure were very with it when they hit him.'

'There's a little bit of blood around here,' said Hope.

'Yes, it's come from one of our witnesses. Fell over the body twice, apparently. Scraped her knee. Well, cut it badly. Ambulance attended to her. She's not serious. Just quite a big gash.'

'Fair enough,' said Hope. 'Anything else we can say about him, though, at the moment?'

'Beaten. Like the last one. Some stab wounds. Tortured. Just like the last one.'

Hope stood for a moment and said nothing until Jona prompted her. 'What? What's up?'

'In the last one, he was dumped on the side of the road. We then have Lauren Starr killed because of it. Why, if there's another body dumped here? Or do we have somebody who thinks everyone's cheating on him or her? Doesn't make sense, like Lauren Starr.'

'You think these could be a copycat, then? And the other one's a closed case all in itself?'

'No,' said Hope. 'I think these dumped bodies are a series. Look at the road again. Look where it is. Major disruption. Always a major disruption. The killer wants this to be seen. This says, we want you to know who this is. We want everybody to be aware of what's happened to them. After all, they handed the ID on a plate. They gave us a way of recognising who the last one was. Finding him quickly. I don't think Perry will have any problems with that ID, either.'

'You told Macleod about this theory?'

'Seoras? Seoras is well ahead,' said Hope. 'He's thinking there's set-ups or something going on. It bothers me though.'

'Why?' asked Jona.

'Because if they're trying to tell us something, we have been told something in the last couple of cases. I thought that something was behind us. I'm wondering now.'

Hope returned to the forensic wagon and took off her coverall suit. She looked around and saw Ross standing beside his car, waving her over.

'Spoke to our three witnesses. You can talk to them in a bit. They're in a mess in a police car. But I've got to be honest, they're not involved. I've had them breathalysed as well. Two of them were pissed as farts,' said Ross.

'Deeply inebriated,' said Hope, 'just for the report.'

'The third one's not as bad as the other two, but she was the one who was driving. Still over the limit, though. And I think that's why she didn't see the body. The other one fell over it twice as well. It's like a comedy of errors out here,' said Ross.

'Doesn't look much like a comedy to me. The body's been beaten, though, Ross,' said Hope. 'Dead before the car hit him. Well dead.'

'You think he was dumped again? Jona say anything about that?'

'With the bruising and wounds on him, it might be quite hard for her to say that straight away, that he was dropped onto the road. I mean, last time, she didn't have to prove it. There was a witness. No witnesses tonight. Probably an easier job to do it without witnesses. I don't think last time they were intending to get spotted.'

'Well,' said Ross, 'we can check CCTV. We can put a call out for drivers who were coming this way. It must have happened not long before the girls were here, though,' he said. 'Talking to Jane Farrow, who was the one that was driving. She pulled off the road at one point. Jane, a bit drunk, was struggling to go at thirty miles an hour. The reason she hit him was she was so focused on trying to drive at fifty so nobody would stop her, that she wasn't watching the road that well. But she said when she pulled in previously, a car went past her. So, the van or whoever's dropped him has got to have done it between that car and Jane Farrow's arrival.'

'Unless, of course, they saw the van. I take it she didn't see what the other car looked like and was it definitely a car?'

'She said a car. I'll double-check with her.'

'Tell me something, Ross,' said Hope. 'Are you getting a feeling about this at all?'

'You not wanting to talk to Perry?' said Ross. 'He does feelings. He does theories and notions. I just do data.'

'No, not like that. Do you not feel it's becoming similar to some of our previous cases, like recent ones?'

'In what way?'

'Two victims, their ID basically handed to us on a plate. This has caused a problem this morning. It's going to be major news. Statement being made.'

'Suppose,' said Ross. 'I think we need to get more on that decal for the van. There could be an angle we could go at, probably one they weren't expecting. They have tried to cover their tracks well but that might be a slip. Whoever it is, I'd like to know what this guy has got to do with MacTavish and Lauren Starr. Unless he turns out to live next door or has been seen around Lauren before, I'm not getting what she has to do with anything.'

Perry returned suddenly.

'You get something?' asked Hope.

'I did. And very quickly. As soon as I called down to the station, they suspected something.'

'What do you mean?' asked Hope.

'Well, the thing is—we're trying to confirm, and we'll get

91

pictures and that—but Sean Devereaux on the ID matches a Sean Devereaux who was the grandfather of a baby girl taken from her pram yesterday.'

'Really?' said Hope. 'But we don't know it's definitely him yet.'

'It's the same name. And MacTavish matched,' said Perry. 'I'm getting a feeling about this. Something says there's a lot more to it. Feeling we're getting told something, or we're about to get schooled.'

'See,' said Ross. 'He's the one with the feelings.'

'I'll get a photo to Jona,' said Perry, 'and see if I can get a match from Uniform without talking to the family. Bit of a delicate matter if it is them.'

'Okay,' said Hope. 'Do that. Let me know how you get on.'

'You want to come and talk to the girls?' asked Ross.

'I'll be over in five minutes.' Hope picked up her phone and called Macleod.

'Yes, Seoras. What's the crisis?'

'Seoras, it's Hope. I'm standing out by the airport on the main road. Another dead body beaten to pulp, tied, ID presented to us on a plate. Thing is, we believe he's Sean Devereaux. Sean Devereaux was also the name of the grandfather of a baby that was kidnapped yesterday in Inverness.'

'Okay.'

'Okay? Is that all you're saying? Perry thinks we're about to be schooled.'

'Schooled?' queried Macleod. 'Not just being told a message?'

'No, he said schooled.'

Macleod went silent for a moment before replying. 'Could very well be right, Hope. He could very well be right.'

Chapter 12

Hope McGrath picked up her phone, standing out on the road by the airport. It would be a long while until the traffic could travel this way again, but she would leave the scene soon. She needed to talk to whoever was running the case on the missing babies. And to get clarification that the Sean Devereaux on the ID was indeed Sean Devereaux, the grandfather of the missing child.

Given what happened last time, she thought it best if Macleod accompanied her. There'd be a DCI on the case for the missing babies. Especially with two of them missing.

'This is Seoras.'

'I'm just about done out here by the airport, Seoras. Do you want to come with me? I need to speak to someone about this missing babies case. We believe Sean Devereaux is the same one who is the grandfather of the missing baby girl.'

'DCI Alex Barnfield's running that now,' said Macleod. 'He got assigned as it's being escalated now the second one's gone.'

'I thought that might be the case. Do you want to come out with me? Might just be easier having a DCI versus DCI meeting, as opposed to myself. He'll see his as top-level?'

'Maybe it is,' said Macleod. 'But I certainly don't want to talk to him. I don't think I'll help your case.'

'Why?' asked Hope. 'This isn't about me doing things myself. I actually think this is a good idea. Getting a DCI on board to speak to a DCI.'

'And I think it's a good idea as well. Except it's the wrong two DCIs,' said Macleod. 'Alex Barnfield came out of Edinburgh. I've actually crossed paths with him before. He's, well . . . you might be better at charming him for help than I will. Very old school. Ancient, in fact.'

'When you say old school, what do you mean by that?'

'Well, he doesn't like me. Because he's very by the book.'

'You're not exactly a maverick,' said Hope.

'Compared to him, I am. But I warn you, he is very old school. You're probably not his kind of detective, either.'

'Well, thanks for that one. I'll fight my own battles shall I?'

'Let's put it this way,' said Macleod. 'He's quite happy with women in the force, just not too high up.'

'I'll take Perry with me then, shall I?'

'No, don't take Perry! Perry was on my team when I had the run-in with him. He'll remember Perry. Take Susan.'

'Not Ross?' asked Hope. 'Ross has got a lot more experience—'

'Ross certainly wouldn't be his type of detective. He never said it out loud, but Ross will not be his type of detective.'

'He's that much of a dinosaur?'

'You're talking to Mr Progressive on the phone,' said Macleod.

'Okay,' said Hope. If Seoras was a progressive, this guy must have been from the ark. She closed the call and looked around for Susan.

'Susan, come here a minute,' and spied Perry behind her. 'Perry, you and Ross are going to finish up here, and then back to the station. We'll catch you later. Susan, you're coming with me. Apparently, DCI Alex Barnfield is now running the missing babies' case. So, we're going to go over and see if our Sean Devereaux matches up with his.'

'Alex Barnfield?' queried Perry.

'You know him?' said Hope, not giving up Macleod's warning from earlier.

'Oh yes,' said Perry. 'Don't mention Macleod. He won't like that.'

'Well, my name's kind of synonymous with Macleod these days.'

'Yes,' said Perry. 'I'll definitely finish up here with Ross.'

The two women got into the car, Susan driving. As she turned on the engine to drive away, Susan turned to Hope.

'What do you think about people within the force getting together?'

'What?' said Hope.

'People within the force. Do you think it's a bad idea?'

'How much time have you got on your hands?' asked Hope.

'Well, not much, really,' said Susan.

'Exactly. Imagine two of you with little time on your hands.'

'You suppose,' said Susan. 'Is that why you went outside, because you knew John wouldn't be busy?'

'I went with John because I love John. John makes me laugh. John makes me feel like me. And just me, and me is enough. He doesn't look at me and see a pin-up girl for the force.' Hope stopped for a moment. 'Well, he does see that side, too. He's a man, after all. But John sees me for me and is happy with me being me. And in fact, he wants me to be me.'

But Susan was somewhere else now, looking out of the window as she drove. 'I guess so,' said Susan, not really listening to Hope.

The drive took about twenty minutes, and when they parked up outside the Devereaux house, Hope emerged first from the car. There were several uniformed officers there. Hope went to speak to the first one, but a man stepped out of the house and started marching towards her. He put his hand up, and so Hope put hers up too, and waited for him until he stepped outside of the small gate on the perimeter of the house grounds.

The man wore a heavy suit that blended into the background. His shoes were black, polished, and were solid. His tie was sombre, but then again, so was the entire outfit. He had hair that was struggling to cover his head, and glasses that sat on the edge of his nose.

'You must be DCI Alex Barnfield. It's good to meet you, sir.' Barnfield reached his hand over and shook Hope's.

'I know you by reputation, McGrath. Bit of a golden girl. And I'm sure it's well deserved,' said Barnfield. 'Why are you here?'

'You may or may not be aware, sir, that I'm currently investigating deaths on the road, or rather, bodies being dumped on the roads around Inverness. We've had one dumped just outside the airport last night. His name is Sean Devereaux. We were just waiting to see if he was Sean Devereaux, the grandfather of your missing girl.'

Barnfield nodded. 'They said that someone popped by on MacTavish as well.'

'Yes. The MacTavish child. It was her uncle that was on the road. Could be a coincidence. So, I'm just looking to try to see, first of all, if Sean Devereaux is the grandfather. Obviously, I don't want to disturb the family more than I have to at this particular time.'

'You got a photo?' said Barnfield.

'Yes.' Hope took out her phone and showed the image of the dead man to him.

'Oh, that's him. That's Sean Devereaux, all right. Look. I don't really want you talking to Alice Devereaux, the mother. She's too emotional to make any sense. And to be honest, from what I've gathered, she's all but estranged from her grandfather. They don't talk; there's no communication. So, I'm not sure you're going to get much out of her.

'We really need to be working together to make sure that she's cared for, looked after, and we get enough information so we can get her child back. I know murder cases get a lot of press, and you'll have all of the kerfuffle with the motorists getting diverted, but I'm sure you'll agree that the work I'm doing will trump yours. Despite the fact that your face probably fits better on the news than mine, I have babies missing.'

'I don't really care whose face fits on the news,' said Hope. 'I'm just trying to get what I can to solve my case.'

'Of course,' said Barnfield. 'Trouble is the press. I don't know what it's been like for you in your career. Maybe you're more used to the press treating you well. But it's not about that. It's not about glamour girls on the press, is it?'

'There's one thing I've never been with the press is a glamour girl,' said Hope. 'When Macleod had me do the press conferences, it was because he knew I could handle them.'

'Yes, well.' Hope noticed Barnfield was looking beyond her, staring now at Susan Cunningham. 'That's the young lady who lost her leg, isn't it?'

'Yes,' said Hope. 'It's DC Cunningham.'

'Oh, she looks like a right piece of work,' he said. Hope wasn't quite sure what he meant by that, but he certainly wasn't taking his eyes off her. 'Macleod certainly runs a diverse team these days. I hear he's even got Ross in with him.'

'Macleod picks his people, the ones he thinks can solve cases,' said Hope, refusing to take the bait. 'You don't mind if I have a quick word?'

'Well, I'd rather you didn't,' said Barnfield. 'She's currently one of our key witnesses. I don't want her disturbed. But I'll tell you anything she tells me. Obviously, if you think she was involved in the Devereaux murder, I can reappraise, but I don't see that at the moment, her child being taken.'

'A very bizarre connection for two babies to be kidnapped and relatives killed.'

'Exactly,' said Barnfield. 'Although you have a third unrelated body, don't you? I will obviously forward anything relevant to you.'

'If you would, I'm not sure yet that the two cases are unrelated.'

'I'm not of that mind,' said Barnfield. 'But we're agreed to share. There, you can tell Macleod that you've sorted me out.'

'With all due respect,' said Hope, 'I won't tell Macleod I've sorted anything out. I'll just update him like I should.'

'Good,' said Barnfield. 'As long as we get some sensible policing. Our Assistant Chief Constable, he's very forward with his policies these days. Seems to be more about the press than about actual getting back to solving crimes.'

'Maybe,' said Hope. 'But if I'm not going to be interviewing Alice Devereaux, I'll head off; at least, now I know who my dead man is. I'll say good day to you, sir,' said Hope.

She was using the 'sir' deliberately, and the man seemed to enjoy it. Before Hope turned, she noticed Barnfield was watching Susan walking back to the car. She didn't like him, but maybe he was a good cop. Still, there was no reason for not changing, not getting more in tune with today. Macleod had, after all, in the main. He certainly tried.

Susan began driving the car back towards the station. As they stopped at a red light, she suddenly turned to Hope.

'What do you make of Tanya?' asked Susan.

'Macleod's PA? What do you mean, what do I make of her?'

'What do you make of her? She's quite attractive, isn't she?'

'She's doing well. I mean, she's lively, from what I've seen. But you need to be to be a PA to Macleod. You need to have that force to stand up for yourself.'

'Do you think older men, they go for that, rather than the sort of more excitable, younger woman?'

'Don't ask me what men go for. I've got John, and I'm quite happy with him. Beyond that, I don't care. I had some men who went for the wrong thing in me. Now, I've got one who wants me. I'm quite happy,' said Hope. 'I'm not the one to ask for advice. Ask Clarissa. She's got an older man.'

'She's got an old man,' said Susan. 'Not an older man. There's no age gap between them, is there?'

'I suppose not,' said Hope. 'What do you want to know for?'

'Nothing,' said Susan. 'Nothing in particular.'

The car went quiet. The lights turned to green, and the car drove off again. A little further along the road, Susan spoke up again. 'I suppose that would work well, wouldn't it? Somebody being in the force and somebody being a PA.'

'Is there a point to this?' said Hope.

'Just thinking.'

'Look,' said Hope. 'I don't mind you thinking, and if push comes to shove, and two people on my team got together, we'll see how we go. But it can't affect the job.'

'Right,' said Susan, and put her head back into driving. It was another two minutes of silence before Susan spoke again. 'Do you think Perry rescued me because I was a colleague? Or do you think Perry rescued me—'

'Can you pull in a minute?' said Hope.

Susan pulled the car over and Hope turned to face her.

'I've got a murder case on my hands, okay? Three dead bodies. I'm struggling to find who did it. Also, I'm pregnant. I wake up every morning and vomit my guts out. And then another couple of times during the day. I've also had to see a complete dinosaur and try to work with him, across two cases. And now you want me to give agony aunt advice to you about whether you and Perry should get together?'

'I didn't say it was Perry.'

'You did say it was Perry. You basically told me it was Perry. If you're worried about Tanya and Perry, talk to Perry. If you're worried about you and Perry, talk to Perry, okay? As far as did Perry come and get you for being a colleague or being a person, Perry would go in there and get any of us. Perry thinks nothing about himself. Perry acts and Perry would get anyone in there. Am I saying that Perry doesn't like you? Of course he likes you. Please get a grip,' said Hope. 'Okay? Tanya clearly likes Perry. If you like Perry, go get him, girl. Otherwise, stop bugging me. I've got enough on my plate.'

'Sorry,' said Susan. 'There's nobody else I can really talk to about it.'

'Plenty of other women on the team.'

'Not on our team,' said Susan.

'You got Sabine in the station. You've got Clarissa. And I'm sure there's plenty of women more your age you can talk to.

However, you deal with it,' said Hope. 'Just deal with it, okay? Between you and me, discussion about Perry as a potential partner is off limits.'

'Fine,' said Susan, and started the car up again. Hope hadn't meant to be so brutal. But at the end of the day, Susan needed to know. Perry and Susan had to work together with no hindrance. Hope needed that to be a fact. Not something she was concerned about.

Chapter 13

Having been told by Hope that she got little from her visit to the Devereaux household, Perry went to the accountancy firm where Sean Devereaux worked. The man had been an accountant for years, as they told Perry on the phone. But Perry thought a visit was a better idea to get the lowdown on just what the man's life was like. Also, he read people better in person.

On the phone, people didn't always tell you the truth, or at least didn't give away as much as they knew. Sometimes it was out of politeness, not out of a willingness to hide anything. But it was always easier if you could read their faces, and you could prompt, look for deeper knowledge, or you could take the real meaning behind the words.

The accountancy firm was on the high street of Inverness. Perry parked the car in one of the multi-storeys and made his way there, but he walked with quite a heavy heart. He was troubled. Susan's affection had been something he had longed for, but it never had come. He'd convinced himself that was okay, and then, when he'd seen Tanya down in Glasgow, he'd been encouraged that she was still interested.

Now he had two women interested in him, and Perry found he didn't like that. He should wallow in it, he thought, but no.

The trouble was, he liked them both. They were very different, and the last thing he wanted was to hurt either of them. On the other hand, it wasn't like he just could decide, pick one, and that was it.

He hadn't sought their affections on him at all, at least not recently. They'd just decided that they liked him. Still, there was work to do, so Perry plodded on until he reached the accountancy firm's front door. Opening it, he swept into a modern office and stood politely until a young lady from behind a desk approached him.

'How can I help you, sir?' she said.

'I'm DC Warren Perry. Spoke on the phone earlier to some of your colleagues. I think they're expecting me.'

He pulled out his warrant card. The young girl smiled and led him through to an office in the back. A tall woman, thin and rather gaunt, entered the office a few moments later and sat down on the large leather chair behind the desk.

'Nice to meet you, Detective Constable,' said the woman. 'How can I help you?'

'Well, I'm looking, as I said on the phone, to find out a bit more about Sean Devereaux. So, I got told a few things, but really I'd like to know a lot more about him.'

'Well, my name's Mary Johnson. I'm one of the lead partners in the firm. And Sean worked with me quite a lot.'

'You were Sean's senior in the firm?' asked Perry.

'He'd worked here a long time, so yes, he had a degree of seniority, but he wasn't a partner. He never reached that level. To be honest, I'm not sure he wanted to. Trouble was,' said Mary, 'that Sean was a tragic figure. His only grandchild, Alice, well, she wouldn't speak to him. And his wife and son died.'

'They died? How?' asked Perry.

'They died in a fire at the house. A lot of Sean's home office at the time was burnt down. Sean was being investigated. Not regarding this accountancy firm, I hasten to add, but regarding some private work he was doing. We'd introduced him to the accounts, but the investigation was specifically to do with his work, not ours.'

'Why, was there something dodgy about it?'

'Dodgy is a very awkward word to use in accountancy firms,' said Mary. 'Let's say I wasn't too happy about some of the business that was going through the accounts. We decided not to offer our services, but Sean did some private work as well, and so we passed it on.'

'So, what was happening?' asked Perry.

'He said it was a hard time for him. He was getting heavily investigated, looking for some financial irregularities, and then his home office burnt down. Wife killed, son killed. A lot of his paperwork had gone too?'

'The paperwork that was being investigated.'

'Yes. Computers burnt up. The storage systems in those days weren't the same as they are now.'

'Did you think there was anything untoward?'

'If I thought Sean was crooked,' said the woman, 'Sean wouldn't be working with me. Anyway, as an accountancy firm, you have to be particularly careful. Follow all your checks. They'd all been done and Sean was signed off. Sean Devereaux was a tragic figure, but I wouldn't have said he was an illicit one.'

'The accounts that were being investigated,' said Perry, 'do you know who any of them were?'

'Well,' said the woman, 'I don't have the specific details of the accounts. I know who we passed on to him and who he took up. We were aware of that so we wouldn't impede each other, so to speak. We needed to delineate what contact had been made with our firm since we'd been approached, and what we'd passed on. So we would have a list of that. It'll be in some of the hard storage. Just a second.' The woman stood up and exited the office, leaving Perry to sit there.

He looked around. His office at the station wasn't like this one. In the far corner was one of those wooden globes. A large one, which he thought might have a decanter or two of whisky hidden inside. He wanted to get up off the chair and spin the globe, but if the lady walked back in, it wouldn't really cut a professional look.

There were a couple of photographs on the wall of Mary at golf events. He thought he recognised one or two of the golfers who were there as well, although he wasn't sure. Perry wasn't that big on sport, despite having played in the police football leagues down in Glasgow.

There were also several qualifications on the wall, which he thought were diplomas or degrees. He stood up and went to look at them. He read through them and was still scanning them when Mary entered.

'I can assure you I'm completely kosher,' she said. 'If you want, you can contact the financial authority. They'll advise you I am who I say I am.'

'No, no,' said Perry, 'that wasn't what I was doing. I was just looking around your office. Saw the qualifications and thought I'd look at them. I don't have mine hanging on the wall. I don't actually have walls around my desk. It's kind of in the middle of a big office. Sorry, I was just feeling a little jealous.'

The woman smiled, but looked at him rather oddly, which

Perry thought was probably fair.

'I obtained a list of those firms for you,' said Mary, and placed it down on the desk. Perry sat back in his seat and looked at them. It was quite an extensive list, covering two pages.

'You gave all of these accounts to him?'

'Over the years,' said Mary, 'that's not the work of five minutes. These clients have approached us over the years and these are the ones that we've passed on. The earlier ones are first.'

'Do you know which of these he still had as clients?'

'No,' said Mary. 'Once he took them on, that was his business. I had no right to see any of the records after that.'

Perry began running down the list. 'It says here a Lord Bairstow,' said Perry. 'The Lord Bairstow that owns the estate west of Inverness?'

'Same one,' said Mary.

'And you didn't take him on? I'd have thought that someone like that would have been an ideal client. Plenty of work.'

'If you look,' said Mary, pointing down, 'it says Lord Bairstow, but it's Pear Holdings. It was only one part of his business that he'd come with. I'm not sure why he had put no other business our way, but he was quite keen. I remember the conversation as I was closer to the work at the time. It didn't really fit what we wanted to do, and I knew Sean was more than capable, so I passed him to Sean.'

'So do you know anything else about Pear Holdings?'

'You're looking at the sum total of what I know. I didn't ask Sean about any of the business we passed to him. That was his decision to take it. He had the interview with the potential client after we had had ours. We'd said no; that was that. Move the client on.

'You see, even if you reject someone as a client for yourself, if you can give them to someone else and they're happy, they look favourably on you,' said Mary. 'Therefore, it was in our best interest to find them somebody who could do the job, but who was still acting independently. But if they were happy, they knew we'd recommended it, and therefore they could come back to us on another date, maybe with an account that was more suitable for us.'

'I see,' said Perry.

The woman sat, expecting another question, but Perry had rocked back in the chair and was pondering.

'Is there anything else I can help you with?' said the woman. 'I'm quite happy to assist you, but I also have work to get on with. So, I don't mean to be rude, Detective Constable, but I don't have time to just have an idle chat. If you need somewhere to think things over, I'm sure I can find you a desk outside.'

'Sorry,' said Perry. He stood up, pulled at his jacket, almost smoothing it down, and then reached forward and shook hands with the woman. 'Thank you, Mary,' he said, before picking up the two pieces of paper he'd been given. 'You've been most helpful. I'm sorry for the loss of Sean from your firm. I'm sure it's a trying time for you all.'

'Of course,' said Mary. 'More of a trying time for his grandchild, Alice. I hear her baby's been kidnapped as well.'

'Terrible business,' said Perry. 'It really is.'

He left and was walking back to the car when he decided he needed to think for a moment. He found a coffee shop, stepped inside, ordered a cortado and sat down. Perry took out his phone and tapped in Pear Holdings. He found the company record but the firm was now wound up.

It had operated only for a couple of years before being closed down. Lord Bairstow was indeed associated with the company. Perry wondered if it had been the one that had been investigated. Bairstow was who MacTavish had worked for, also Lauren Starr; two dead bodies. Now the third body, Sean Devereaux, was also linked to Bairstow. That didn't sound like a coincidence, but was certainly something that he had to look into. He picked up his phone and placed a call into the station. It was picked up by Ross.

'Ross, I've got an issue. Sean Devereaux was an accountant. He worked at a firm in town. However, he ran some accounts on his own. One of the accounts that he ran belonged to Lord Bairstow. The business, Pear Holdings, however, is now defunct. It was wound up. I believe it may have been investigated. I'm not sure how to take a closer look at that.'

'You need to leave that one with me, Perry. I'll get into that. Not a problem. It'll be best if you make your way back to the office,' said Ross. 'I think the boss wants to pull everybody in and have a chat. See where we're going at the moment. It's been full on. Jona's running around like a headless chicken. We've got the two missing children as well, so the place is a buzz. Just watch out for the press when you come in. If you can knock a few of them down, it'll be fine by me.'

'I'll do my best,' said Perry.

He closed down the call and thought Ross sounded a little agitated. It wasn't like him to comment like that. Knock the press down. Perry had thought about it in his life. Unfortunately, his career would be over if he did so.

He finished up his cortado and walked back to his car. As he got inside, he felt his shoulders slumping in. He would have to do something about Susan and Tanya.

But what? What would he do? Neither of them had . . . well, actually they had, hadn't they? Tanya implicitly had. That's why she was up here. There was a chance. There was a hope. A flicker. She'd said so much. And now she said that she would knock Susan out of the way if Susan was the one after Perry.

He wasn't used to this, being the centre of attention. Perry thought about Tanya and the times they'd had in the past. He'd been a bit younger then. And they'd been fun. And she was quite wonderful.

So was Susan. Susan was the stranger of the two women for Perry to be interested in. She was younger. What struck Perry was it wasn't just her physical looks that grabbed him. She was gorgeous—of course, she was. Tanya was too, even if she was older. But Perry found he warmed to Susan. They got on easily. They worked well together.

Tanya had always picked Perry up, always been the one to shake him down, always been the one to drag Perry around. And he enjoyed it. He really did. Susan, however, was more subtle, easier, companionable. Was that the word he was looking for? Was that what he wanted, a companion? It sounded like an old word. Was he old? Perry wasn't sure. Perry wasn't sure of a lot of things at the moment.

Perry started the car, put it in reverse and pulled out of his parking space. As he descended the multi-storey, heading back to the office, he put on the radio. There was a song playing. A song that reminded him of Glasgow. A song that told him of times with Tanya. Was Tanya just a period of time he wanted to get back? Because that never worked, did it? Was Susan the reality now?

He wouldn't know. With love and affection, Perry wasn't the greatest of detectives.

Chapter 14

What on earth was going on? One of the main roads out of Inverness, which ran by the railway line, was blocked solid. It couldn't have happened that long ago because it would back up really quickly for it was a busy road.

Perry slammed the wheel. Hope was having a meeting, and he didn't want to arrive late. That wouldn't do. Now he was stuck here. There were cars in front of him and now cars had blocked him from behind. He was going nowhere. He sat there for a couple of minutes, and then he picked up his mobile phone, calling the station.

'DC Perry here. Anything going on that I should know about in town?'

'It's just the road's blocked, coming out from the centre. Up towards the roundabout for the hospital. We just had calls. There should be officers on their way down. Apparently, there's a body on the road.'

Perry opened the car door, and then slammed it behind him. He was still holding the phone as he ran. 'A body? What sort of body?'

'A dead one,' said the desk sergeant.

'Well, I'm here. I'm going to it. You can get anyone who

needs to phone me.'

Perry closed the call and continued to half jog. He didn't know how far ahead it was and Perry wasn't the greatest at running. He wasn't unfit, but neither was he a sprinter.

As Perry got closer to the corner ahead, he could see that the line of cars ended. Some people were out of their cars and screaming. Perry raced to them.

'I'm Detective Constable Warren Perry.' As he said the words, he saw the body lying on the floor. It was female, naked, and was heavily battered. He saw a woman close to him, faint. A man tried to grab her as she went to the floor.

'Ambulance. That woman will need an ambulance. Call it now,' he said, pointing at one man.

He stepped forward, pulling out some gloves from inside his jacket pocket. Having donned them, he reached down and checked the woman's pulse lying on the floor. Well, she was dead all right. Cold. He looked around the body and then saw she was holding a purse in her hand. In the distance, Perry could hear the police sirens and, now down on his knees, he turned and told everyone to take a step back.

The woman must have been somewhere around fifty, Perry thought, and had short-cut black hair. He pulled at the purse that was in her hand, but it was tucked tight and he had to pull hard. Once it was out, he opened it. Inside was a card. It said *Sylvia White, Hairdresser*. It gave a number along with an address.

Perry reached round into his jacket, pulled out an evidence bag, and dropped the purse into it. He then realised that some of the uniformed officers had arrived.

'Let's get this all cordoned off. Get a hold of your colleagues. You need to stop anybody else coming down this road,' he said, 'and then we'll need to move these cars around and away. We'll also need to get a tent or something down to cover this body before we take everybody past it.'

The constable he was talking to nodded and spoke into the radio. Perry stepped back. He heard ambulance sirens. The paramedics would need to get up close soon. Perry felt his phone vibrate. He picked it up and saw that Hope was looking for him.

'This is Perry. I'm on scene. It's another one,' he said to Hope. 'This is Sylvia White. Had a purse in her hands. I've got it in an evidence bag.'

'I'll be down. On my way,' said Hope. 'Any other detail about her?'

'Got an occupation and address.'

'Phone Ross. Tell him to find out who she is.'

'Will do,' said Perry. He called Ross.

'I'm just on the way out the door,' said Ross.

'Boss wants you to check this. Sylvia White.' And he passed the address and phone number. 'See if you can find out who she is.'

'Do you need any further assistance down there?' asked Ross.

'The boss will be here soon. I assume Susan's coming with her. Once Jona gets here, she can take over. I think we're okay. I've got plenty of uniform arriving now. It's right smack in the middle of the main road out of town. A major obstruction, like the other two. It's going to get noticed. And they're telling us who it is.'

'Okay,' said Ross. 'I'll get on it.'

Perry closed down the call and stepped back. He turned to some people who were still standing there. Most had moved away now. A dead body was uncomfortable to look at. Especially a naked one—one that looked like it had the tripe beaten out of it.

'Are you one of the first people to come across the body?' asked Perry, talking to one driver.

'Yes, sir. Yes, I am.'

'How was it? Just lying here? Did somebody dump it?'

'I was towards the front. That's my car, two back. We were down at the lights, and we were being held. But those coming out of the supermarket car park didn't come out, either. Some guy was crossing the road where the supermarket exit came out. It meant that none of those cars came.'

'Really?' said Perry. 'Did you notice any of the cars that were ahead? The cars that went before you, that obviously didn't see the body.'

'Well, there was a van,' the man said. 'Red and white.'

'Can you describe the van?' asked Perry.

'I just did,' he said, 'red and white.'

'No, no,' said Perry. 'What size of van? Small one? Could you stand up in the back of it?'

'Sort of transit size,' said the man.

Perry continued to ask those standing around. He was getting the same message. An incident back at the previous traffic lights had caused the issue. He'd need to check drivers coming the other way. Were they held up, or did they see the van? He assumed the van dropped the body again. But this one was red and white. Did they have different decals? It was a clever way of covering their tracks.

Perry heard a shout and turned to see Hope arriving. A forensic wagon was coming too, and he watched as Jona Nakamura jumped out and started barking orders to everyone, securing her scene. Hope raced over to Perry.

'Dear God, Perry. Another one.'

'They've beaten her. Really beaten her. She's dead, though. Definitely dead.'

'Any idea what happened?'

'Well, I think we're going to cordon off about the first five or six cars in each lane here to get the details. I'll interview these people. What I've picked up so far is that they got held back at the lights up near the supermarket. Those coming out from the supermarket got held as well by some idiot crossing the road when they were meant to be going. What they're saying, though, is that there was a transit van that was the last thing to go down the road. Red and white.'

'Red and white,' said Hope.

'Susan's thing about the decals. I think she's right. Think about it. A great way to keep changing up the van.'

'It certainly is,' said Hope.

Perry looked over Hope's shoulder and saw Susan Cunningham now approaching. She'd probably come down in the car with Hope and had been parking it out of the way. As she approached, she smiled at Perry.

'You okay?' asked Susan.

'Yes,' said Perry. 'We've got another victim. Sylvia White. Ross is looking her up, see if we can find more on her. She had a purse in her hands, got details from that.' He watched as Jona Nakamura came over.

'Who got here first?' asked Jona.

'That's me,' said Perry. 'My car's still in this load behind you here. When I got here, she was like she is now, except there was a purse in her hands.'

'A purse?'

'Yes,' said Perry. He pulled out an evidence bag from his jacket pocket and handed the purse over. 'Sylvia White, card inside, hairdresser. Address, phone number on it.'

'Anything else?'

'No, except she's tied up like that.'

Jona disappeared for a moment before coming back in a coverall suit and began to approach the body. Perry watched Hope go to follow her, but Jona waved at her, pushing her back.

'Keep everybody off the road here, just in case there's any tyre marks. Perry, can you make sure your uniform has sealed the entire place? These cars don't want to come down the other side either. Keep them clear of that for the moment. If we're dispersing them, they want to be going backwards.'

'You've done traffic before,' said Perry, 'because you don't make it easy.'

Jona gave him a half grin and then turned to look over the body. Hope stood on the pavement with Susan and Perry. A sergeant from Uniform approached.

'Inspector?' he said to Hope.

'Just Hope will do. Get the area secured. Jona's asked that these cars go backwards. I want the name and address of everybody in them, though. And get a message out. We want to see if we can get whoever was coming down the other way.'

'Of course.'

Hope turned to Susan. 'CCTV. Got to be some here. You're looking for a red and white van. Possibly similar to what you picked out before.'

'Red and white,' said Susan.

'They said that was the last vehicle that went down here. A red and white van. They've probably got red decal on this time.'

Susan nodded and disappeared.

'What do you make of it, Perry? Three dead bodies on the road.'

'They're not three dead bodies, they're three offerings. They're talking to us, aren't they? Look at these people. Have a proper look at them. Oh, by the way,' said Perry, 'I went to see about Sean Devereaux's accountancy firm. Turns out that he had an account with Lord Bairstow. Pear Holdings. He was running it for him. It's now defunct. I've got Ross looking into that as well,' said Perry. 'He's better at that sort of thing. But apparently Pear Holdings was being investigated. Sean Devereaux's house burnt down. Wife and son died. Alice won't talk to him now.'

'Bairstow was involved in this. We need to see if Bairstow's got any connection to this woman.'

'She's quite toned though, isn't she?' said Perry, looking over at the body.

'I'm sorry?' said Hope.

'I said she's quite toned, that woman.' Perry paused for a moment. He was looking at a cadaver and saying how toned it was. 'Not that I'm commenting about her, I'm just saying she looks for her age to be in fantastic condition.'

'So?' said Hope.

'She's a hairdresser, and she looks in great condition. Most hairdressers, especially at the older age, don't get me wrong, they don't look, well . . . they're not walking around all day, so they rarely look in such great shape. By that stage of life, you don't keep in that sort of shape. She's got muscle in her arms. Muscle in the legs.'

Hope nodded. 'You're right. She could just be a fitness nut

for all we know.'

'She could be,' said Perry, 'but . . . coincidence? Our last two weren't in good shape. She is. But then the last one was an accountant. Didn't expect him to be in top shape. MacTavish. Well, MacTavish was a worker for Bairstow. This woman, the hairdresser, and she's in good shape. I'm not saying it's anything definite. I'm just saying.'

'Okay,' said Hope. Perry felt his phone vibrate again and picked it up.

'It's Ross here. Perry, that Sylvia White. What ID did she have on her?'

'Well,' said Perry, 'I got a card, her hairdressing card. That's where the phone number was from. But I got the address off her driving license.'

'Go and get Jona. Get me the driving license number, please.'

Perry called Jona over and while Jona picked out the driving licence from the purse and held it up in front of Perry, he recited the letters and numbers that made up the driving licence number to Ross.

'That's a fake,' said Ross. 'It's not registered on the system. Tell Jona to take good care of that driving licence. Ask her to see if it's made up properly, or if it's a fake. The licence number certainly doesn't add up.'

'Did you find anything else, though?'

'Called the number for the hairdressers. Just got a message saying that you could leave your message. I didn't bother, not until we work out more about who she is. It just seems a little strange to me.'

'Doesn't it,' said Perry. He closed the call down and told Hope what Ross had said. He watched as his tall, ginger-haired colleague walked away for a moment, looking around her.

117

Then she turned back to him.

'You need to find a connection between that woman and Lord Bairstow. He's the only thing linking everything up at the moment. Lauren Starr too. Does she have any connections to these other people? Something's not right here. We're being told something. We're being handed it on a plate. Much more so this time than last time. Less cryptic. You get given a driving licence, and it's fake. What does that mean?'

'A person who doesn't live their own life,' said Perry. 'Someone from the shadows. Someone—'

'Agencies,' said Hope. 'Agencies. That's all we need. I'm going to call Macleod. This is all, well, this is all getting far too similar to the case we had last time. Only they're handing it to us. Truly handing it to us. Something about this feels different.'

Perry gave a nod. He had to agree.

Chapter 15

Macleod stood looking out of his window. It always got to him. This one was never as good. Hope's office window was much better. From here, all he could see was the press. He was standing with the blinds turned slightly so that they couldn't see him but he knew if he moved too far, they would.

One problem with contemplation, with looking out of the window, was that anybody looking in thought that you looked lost. That you were out of ideas. At least that's how the press would put it. He couldn't be a DCI who looked out of ideas. Certainly not at the moment. In saying that, Macleod was worried.

There was a rap on the door, and Macleod called for whoever it was to come in. He turned and saw the door open, swinging back before Tanya entered, holding a tray out in front of her. It had a cafetiere of coffee on it, and a single cup beside it.

She approached his desk, and put the cafetiere down, along with the cup.

'I didn't ask for any coffee,' said Macleod.

'I thought you looked like you could do with one.'

'I'm sorry?' said Macleod.

'You looked like you could do with a coffee. Everyone says

you and coffee, it's like an entire relationship.'

'You don't need to make me a coffee just because I appear worried,' said Macleod.

'Actually, I do,' said Tanya. 'That's my job. I'm here to support you. I have to support you in the things that you don't even realise.'

She pushed the plunger down on the cafetiere and then slowly poured the coffee. She took the cup and passed it to Macleod at the window.

He thanked her, took the cup to his lips, and drank. Well, she certainly could make coffee. It had been one of his greatest fears about taking on a new secretary, that they couldn't make a decent coffee. He could make it himself, of course, but that was a funny thing. So many people seemed to say that they should make him the coffee, not the other way round. It was like he was taking their role if he made it.

'This window,' said Macleod. 'It's rubbish.'

'I'm sorry?' said Tanya.

'It's rubbish. It really is. You look out and what can you see?' Tanya stepped forward, but Macleod held a hand up. 'Not too far,' he said, 'lest they see you.'

'Oh, the press. A lot of press about at the moment, isn't there?' said Tanya.

'Yes,' said Macleod. 'I like to think. I like to ponder. You think better when you can see a view, when there's something out there. If you sit in a room and look at the walls, you don't think the same. It's like your mind has to have room to expand.'

'It's funny,' said Tanya.

'What is?' asked Macleod.

'Down in Glasgow, if I can be so rude, they always said you were a grumpy git.' Macleod turned to stare at her. 'I didn't say I said it,' said Tanya. 'They said it.'

'Who's they?'

'Most people. Except your team didn't. Perry's never said that about you.'

'No, what Perry thinks is probably a lot ruder, but Perry wouldn't say it. Perry's good at spotting everybody's little foibles. He can see the bits that don't work on a person. And the bits that do work. He's good like that. He's a deep man. Many people don't see it.'

'He's deep,' said Tanya. 'Brave, too.'

'Daft,' said Macleod. 'He charges in sometimes where he shouldn't.'

'It's only because he cares,' said Tanya. 'He cares too much. He's a sensitive soul underneath.'

Macleod almost reacted to that. Almost asked how much she really knew about him. But that wasn't his business. He kept drinking his coffee.

'Susan and Perry,' asked Tanya. 'What are they like together?'

Macleod laughed. 'I don't care if you brought me coffee. That's not something I go into. I don't see that with people. For all my deductive powers, I don't see how people gel on the more sort of . . .'

'Romantic?' said Tanya.

'Personal level,' said Macleod. He continued to stare out the window.

'Can I be rude?' asked Tanya.

'I'm sure you can,' said Macleod.

'I think you're talking bollocks, Seoras. You see, I think you know fine rightly the situation between the two of them.' Macleod grinned, but he didn't look at Tanya.

'I don't get involved in that side of things,' said Macleod.

121

'If it's not interfering with work, I don't get involved. Is it interfering with work?'

'I don't know,' said Tanya. 'That's why I'm asking about the two of them. I don't know how they are together.'

'I wasn't asking about them. I'm asking about you and Perry.' Tanya almost blushed. 'I really don't mind what people get up to outside of work. And you could do a heck of a lot worse in this life than Perry. I'm very fond of him,' said Macleod. 'As for him and Susan, you have to work that out, not me.' She went to turn away, but Macleod reached across and put his hand on her shoulder.

Tanya turned back. He stared for a moment. She was just perfect as regards a secretary, candid with him, happy to speak her mind, but polite enough to say she was going to do it. She looked imposing and yet warm at the same time. Her hair rolled down onto her shoulders. She had a, well, he had to say attractive blouse on, but not one that was all about the attraction. One that said, I am something. One that said, I also know how to handle myself. She had a skirt that made her figure stand out, and yet didn't say, that's all I am is a figure.

'If you ever need to speak to me,' said Macleod, 'I'm here. You're my PA. You're my assistant. Sometimes things get rough. If they get rough for you, I'm here, okay? I'm very impressed by you. Not just the fact you helped us out previously. But by the way you handle yourself here.'

There was a rap on the door. Tanya turned and looked at Macleod. 'That's the Assistant Chief Constable.'

'Jim,' said Macleod. 'You can tell that's Jim.'

'There was a shuffle of feet before he knocked. When he comes to your office, he almost preps himself before he makes an approach,' said Tanya.

'He does,' said Macleod. He knew it was Jim as well, but he was impressed that she did. 'Let Jim in,' he said. 'Ask him if he wants a coffee. In fact, just bring another cup in. There's plenty there on the desk.'

Tanya approached the door, opened it, and welcomed Jim into the office. She left the door slightly open before returning with a cup and placing it on the desk. Jim, however, didn't take a seat. Macleod gave a nod to Tanya, and she left the office.

'We need to talk, Seoras.'

'Of course,' said Macleod.

'Are we okay in this office? Do you know we are okay?'

Macleod knew his office wasn't bugged, not because he could do that himself, but because of recent days. Kirsten Stewart had been in and checked it. With all that had gone on before, Macleod wanted to make sure that he had places he could talk properly and not worry about what was being said.

'It's okay; we're good, Jim. What's up?' asked Macleod.

'I've been told to advise you that you shouldn't look too heavily into Lord Bairstow, not unless you have the proof.'

'I'm sorry?' said Macleod. 'Lord Bairstow came up in the most recent case, but we're not looking heavily into Lord Bairstow. He's the employer of some people who have died. We visited him to find out about them. We're not pulling in Lord Bairstow.'

'Someone is,' said Jim.

'Why is the chief constable finding out such detail about my murder case? Have you spoken to him about it yet?'

'Briefly. Brief details. It's nothing that out of the ordinary, or at least nothing that I'd expect to be getting information on or being told how to conduct our business. It's not like you don't know how to run a murder investigation . . . or Hope.'

123

Macleod pointed to the seat on the other side of his desk. 'Take a seat, Jim, for a moment. I want to check something.' Macleod picked up his phone and called Hope.

'Yes?' said Hope. 'Kind of busy.'

'Are we looking into Lord Bairstow at the moment?'

'Well, Perry had his name. It was at the accountancy firm that Sean Devereaux worked at. Lord Bairstow's name and a company came up. Ross is having a look at it. But it's a link at the moment. Nothing more, nothing less.'

'Okay,' said Macleod. Macleod then rang Ross downstairs.

'Are you looking into Lord Bairstow?'

'Having a look at Pear Holdings. It's come up with Sean Devereaux.'

'I know, I know,' said Macleod. 'When you say you're having a look, what do you mean?'

'Pear Holdings was getting investigated at the same time as Sean Devereaux had a fire in his house. His wife and his child died. I'm just checking out what the investigation into Pear Holdings was about. It's defunct now; it's in the past.'

'Is anything coming up?'

'Well, there's some interesting stuff, but I'm having to delve deeply.'

'Be careful,' said Macleod. 'I'm getting some heat. It must have come from what you're digging up or what you're looking at.'

'You want me to stop?' said Ross.

'Absolutely not,' said Macleod. 'You dig away, but you dig carefully. Watch your back.'

Macleod put the phone down and looked over at Jim, who was staring back with a worried face.

'This case is a bit brutal,' said Jim, 'but it is a case, a normal one, a murder inquiry. Bairstow wasn't part and parcel of it. The idea that we're getting warned off looking into things doesn't seem right.'

'Jim,' said Macleod, 'can we be candid?'

'Course,' said Jim.

'Things that have gone before—do you think they're gone?'

'You handed it over, didn't you?' said Jim. 'You told Anna Hunt it was hers to look into.'

'She told me they would come back,' said Macleod.

'You think this has got something to do with all of that?'

'I'm beginning to. I'm really beginning to. What bothers me, Jim, is we're getting told by our chief constable to be careful.'

'He's sound,' said Jim. 'He's just passing on. The chief's not—'

'I don't think he is, either,' said Macleod. 'But when higher-up people say things, he's got to be, well, passing the buck down, hasn't he? He's got to at least have said, even if he's got his own suspicions, his own ideas.'

'I don't like this,' said Jim. 'I really don't. Tell your guys to be watching their backs. Be careful. Especially around Bairstow.'

'Our latest victim, if she's tangled up with Bairstow, maybe it'll be another boat that's being rocked. Everything we've got so far has been handed to us. Last time, it was handed to us more cryptically, but it was there. And they killed people. Now it's bothering me because it's not exactly the same.'

'What way?' asked Jim.

'We've got missing children. They're tied into our first two road victims. Our third one. Well, babies are linked in,' said Macleod. 'I can't see why, but they're there. Everything so far has been guilty people. We've got two sides. Ones who ended the lives of people they thought were guilty of crimes. Then there's those who feel that the law has acted above the law and are out to expose that, and have killed people who are guilty of doing that.

'Babies are guilty of nothing, and they haven't been returned, and yet I think they're linked in with those dead bodies, the ones who have been found on the road. That worries me, Jim. The trouble with games is that suddenly everybody gets involved in them, even those who have nothing to do with the game. It's like a war. They always say the first casualty of war is innocence. It's not. It's usually those who weren't even involved, standing by the roadsides.'

Jim looked back up at him. 'Tell your people to be careful. I'll tell the Chief Constable I've passed the message on. You need help with this one, I'm here,' said Jim. He stood up and reached over, and Macleod put his hand out to shake it. 'I know we've had our difficulties in the past. I know I'm not necessarily the policeman you would want me to be, but I'm not one of them, and I'll help you flush it out.'

'Jim, you are who you are. You're certainly a good one. It's good to know you're there.' Macleod watched Jim leave the office before he picked up the phone and called Hope again, telling his team to watch their backs. It was not what you needed on a murder investigation.

Chapter 16

Hope McGrath drove away after making sure that the scene had been dealt with thoroughly. Uniform were taking statements, and Susan would run through those once they were complete. The road was blocked off because Jona was still working with her crew, and Hope had to take a roundabout route back to the station. As she drove, she felt queasy and pulled off into a lay-by on the side of the road to find some toilets. Having done so, she exited the car and walked into what she thought were rather run-down affair. She didn't care though, because her stomach was churning. It hadn't been seeing the body in the road; it was just this morning sickness. It never seemed to leave her.

Hope entered the toilets to find there were three cubicles and instantly rushed to the nearest one. From the corner of her eye, she saw that somebody had entered the toilets behind her. But she didn't care, pushing open the door, dropping to her knees, and throwing up the toilet seat.

'Are you okay?' said the voice behind her.

'Yes,' said Hope, and then promptly vomited into the toilet. She felt a hand rubbing her back.

'Are you okay? It's okay. Take it easy. Get it all out. It's okay.' The person had grabbed Hope's hair too, holding her ponytail out of the way. Hope was sure it probably wouldn't have got in front of her face, but nonetheless, the help was appreciated.

She spent the next couple of minutes waiting, just to see if her stomach would turn over again. And then she slowly raised herself back up. The woman's hand was still rubbing up and down her back, through her leather jacket. A tissue was presented across Hope's face, wiping some sweat. Hope finally turned to look at the woman beside her.

The face was concerned, and was framed with long black hair. The woman wore a leather jacket, similar to Hope's but her face was older. She recognised Anna Hunt.

'You feel better now?' said Anna.

'No,' said Hope. 'Just emptier.'

Anna helped Hope back up to her feet. 'I think maybe we should talk,' she said. 'Preferably not in here. I don't know about you, but quite a vile smell.'

Hope reached forward and flushed the toilet, and Anna went to wash her hands, allowing Hope to do her own. When Hope left the toilets, Anna was standing outside.

'You up for a short walk?' said Anna.

'Do you normally follow people around to the toilets? Or were you just passing in the car and thought that woman needs a bit of help?'

Anna smiled. 'You've just come from a rather disturbing scene. Oh, but by the way, your hair looks fabulous. You're glowing.'

'I'm not in the mood,' said Hope.

'Really? It's going to be a long day.'

'It's been a long couple of days so far.'

'So I hear. I've also heard Sylvia White's dead.'

'Yes,' said Hope. 'Our hairdresser. Our hairdresser with a driving licence that doesn't check out.'

'There's a reason for that,' said Anna. 'Come with me.' She started walking down the street and Hope matched her stride for stride. 'Sylvia is ex-Service,' said Anna.

Hope stared at her. 'Ex-service?'

'Yes.'

'Are you sure about the ex?' said Hope. 'My constable noted how in shape she was, toned, for a woman of her age. I should have clocked it then, what he was saying. Similar to you.'

'A woman of her age,' said Anna. 'I'll try not to take that personally. I doubt your constable would have phrased it that way.'

'He was right though, wasn't he?'

'He was, but she is ex-Service. She may have kept herself fit and on her toes, as so many of my ex-colleagues do. You see, you never really leave the Service, or at least the Service never leaves you. They're always keeping an eye on those who have gone before and made it out. You have to. We train up deadly weapons. People who can think quickly, operate in the dark, hide from others. They have a lot of skills that if given to the wrong people, or used by the wrong hands, could be highly detrimental to the country.'

'Would Sylvia be highly detrimental to the country?' asked Hope.

'On the contrary,' said Anna. 'Sylvia was an excellent agent. She could blend in, she could work people over, get information without them knowing anything about her. Why she'd been there many times in life, she entered situations, came out with what we needed to know and moved on in life as if it was all perfectly normal. That's how good undercover agents operate. You don't even know they've been there.

'You're more used to the idea of Kirsten,' said Anna. 'You send Kirsten in when there's trouble, when you need somebody who can operate, take people out, solve situations. Sylvia wasn't somebody who did that. She was an intelligence gatherer, or she would do very covert operations where nobody would know you were there.'

'And she's dead,' said Hope. 'Dead after being dumped, potentially from a van, on a road, in a similar fashion to two other people, and I take it they weren't Service. My constable never commented to me about their toned bodies.'

'No. Those two weren't ours. The interesting thing,' said Anna, 'is that Sylvia, some time ago, tried to infiltrate a circle.'

'A circle?' said Hope.

'Yes. Untoward things are happening. At least, that was the gist of it. We needed somebody in to check them out. It was a circle involving Lord Bairstow.'

Hope stopped walking. 'So, she's connected to him. The other two were connected to him. So is Lauren Starr. Strange, that one, isn't it? Lauren Starr wasn't dumped out on the road.'

'Hmm. I tend to find, Hope, that if people operate in a mode, they don't operate outside of it. They find something that works, or something that works for their agenda. There's clearly an agenda here, isn't there? You don't stop the traffic in Inverness for no reason. You either bring a lot of grief, or you bring a lot of attention. A lot of attention has been brought to these bodies because of where they've been found. Sylvia White was getting on well in that circle. She was deep in. However, she was pulled away from the investigation.'

'Why?' asked Hope.

'I don't know,' said Anna.

'You're the head of the Service,' said Hope.

'I'm currently the head of the Service. I wasn't the head of the Service then.'

'But you'd have the records, wouldn't you?'

'Doesn't always work like that. Sometimes with the Service, there are no records. The former head, Godfrey,' said Anna, 'pulled her out. Sylvia was a good agent. I worked with her several times. If I'm honest, she may have kept me alive once or twice. Those things happen more often in the Service than you'd think.

'That being said, she had gone. She had stepped out, and yes, she still had her cover, but she wouldn't have carried it like that. Somebody got to Sylvia, and somebody left her for dead, and left you a message about her. She was a wonderful agent, Hope,' said Anna. She put her hand up on Hope's shoulder and looked up towards Hope, the couple of inches in height between the women so clear. 'I want to know why she's dead. She's one of ours. Bairstow has got to be involved.'

'So, she was there. What else can you tell me about it? What else about this circle? You must have had a look. You must have gone to talk to others who were involved in the investigation.'

'That's awkward,' said Anna. 'You may not have realised, but the Service has changed somewhat. A year or so ago, maybe a little more, there was a revolution within the Service. Quite a number of our agents are no longer our agents. I'll not wash my dirty laundry in public or tell you about it. Kirsten was involved. She won't tell you either.

'What I can tell you is that the few who are still on our side said our initial intel about the circle, to investigate Bairstow specifically, was from Simon Matthews. I believe Simon Matthews was named in an investigation carried out by DI

Emmett Grump down in Pitlochry.'

'Simon Matthews was killed after giving information out,' said Hope. 'The group that did a lot of the killings recently did it because people like Simon Matthews were killed. Simon Matthews and others were taken out by a higher-up group who didn't follow the law but chose to enact a law of their own.'

'Indeed. You see, Sylvia, her real name is Harriet Carson, in case it comes up, interviewed Simon Matthews. Information regarding Bairstow being a problem came from Simon.'

'So Simon knew something. Simon was a problem then for the group. No wonder they killed him,' mused Hope.

'Watch your back,' said Anna. 'Moving into a circle like that with Bairstow, you watch your back. Be careful. Godfrey laid off them. My former colleague was the head of the Service for a reason. He didn't trust people, but unlike me, Godfrey was prepared to make compromises far beyond what I would make.'

'The idea we simply go in and kill a civilian in this country because they're making accusations about people operating illegally is not something the Service do. Sometimes we operate to shut people down in the national interest, but we do not operate illegally and on our own agenda. We operate to protect the country. At least I do. Godfrey didn't always see it that way. Therefore, Godfrey made alliances. Maybe Godfrey thought that somebody like Matthews was good to take out.

'Be careful. Be very careful. Macleod said he was out. Said it was up to me to investigate all this. Doesn't look to me that others agree with him. I think they want you back in the game. They're trying to highlight this group. The trouble is, they've gone wrong with Sylvia.'

'So, they think Sylvia was operating with Bairstow?'

'She wasn't. She was undercover in the group. They've got it wrong. Anyway,' said Anna, 'this is my car. Take care. Look after that little one. I hope the sickness goes soon.' Anna went to get into the car and Hope turned to her.

'Thank you.'

'It's in the interest of the country to get this matter dealt with. Both above and below. I told Macleod, I am not the enemy here. I'm a friend. We're on the same side. Sometimes my actions don't match his because I do the things he can't do. We're on the same side and because of that, you're as much a target as me. Take care of yourself.'

Anna got into the driver's seat of the car and drove off, leaving Hope to turn and walk back towards her car.

She needed to get her team together. Who else would be brought up and thrown down on the road? Who else would be highlighted? One thing was obvious, though. The group who were putting the bodies on the road didn't know everything. They only knew what they saw, only knew from a distance. They clearly had never been inside the circle. Sylvia White had. Sylvia White was dead.

It was a shame, because she hoped she could have understood exactly where Lord Bairstow fitted into this. She got in behind the wheel of the car, turned the engine on, and drove off. She felt a brief flutter from down round her stomach. *No*, she thought, *that was lower. Was that a little kick or something?* She smiled to herself, and then she thought of those two missing babies.

It's also why Anna wanted it sorted. Collateral. Innocence being brought in. Hope was sure the babies had something to do with this case. She just wasn't sure why. She couldn't see it. They weren't part of the group. They weren't brought into it. Mere babes of no age. What could the possible point be of having them?

Hope needed to find out. She needed to gather her team. She sent a text out to everyone, requesting that they route back to the station as soon as possible. Hope was going to sort this out. She had to, before things got out of hand.

Chapter 17

H ope stood in the women's restroom, looking in the mirror. She looked tired, even though her hair had such lustre. It had been a rough day, a busy day, and one that had followed several others in a similar vein. She needed to get herself together now, pull the team, and charge forward again.

She had asked Seoras to come down too. It would be important to have him there. He was always good at letting her run the investigation, but she needed his advice on this one. There was too much over and above going on. He would know how to handle that better than she. And Anna Hunt's lot was involved now, too. It always made Hope uneasy.

She splashed water on her face, dried it, and then walked back towards her own offices. On entering, she saw her team sitting at their desks, waiting for her, and she turned into her own office. They followed instantly, and sat down at the round table in the corner of her office, one that had been used to bring everyone together since the days when Macleod had the office.

He wasn't here yet, and they all sat together before Ross disappeared out and made coffee. It seemed you could never stop the man. Macleod was coming. That's why the coffee was coming. Hope was under no illusions it was for her. Ross had never seen Macleod had stepped up, and though Ross was now a sergeant, he still treated Macleod as if he was Macleod's gopher, his boy running around making sure Seoras was okay.

When Macleod did swing in, apologising for being a few minutes late, he sat down to a steaming cup of black coffee. Hope saw Ross glance over, waiting to get that grateful smile from Macleod.

'Maybe you can start us, Alan,' said Hope, 'now that we're together. Lord Bairstow—you were looking into him. What have we got?'

'Well,' said Ross, 'Lord Bairstow had several allegations made against his company. A company that's now defunct, Pear Holdings. There was a belief he was money laundering for another organisation. An organisation that's unnamed in the investigation.'

'What do you mean it's unnamed?' said Macleod.

'Exactly what I say, sir. It's unnamed. They found it difficult to work out exactly where the money was going, but it was going to somewhere specific.'

'So, what happened with the allegations?'

'They started to be investigated and then they were abruptly stopped,' said Ross. 'Simon Matthews also made allegations. That's noted in the investigation. But they're nothing that made good evidence, so the investigation halted. I guess they couldn't throw money after something which was yielding no results.'

'Possibly,' mused Macleod.

'Alternatively,' said Hope, 'the Service were investigating him. I know they were.'

'You think they got involved after?' asked Ross.

'That's how they operate, isn't it?' asked Hope to Macleod.

'That would be certainly something. You can't get in by a normal route, ask the Service to take a look. They'll go in via other routes. Routes that you don't have to produce in a court of law.'

'Well, they did. They investigated it, but then that agent was pulled away,' said Hope.

'Why?' asked Macleod.

'Unknown. I spoke to Anna Hunt today,' said Hope, and noticed Macleod raised an eyebrow. 'She came to me. Anna said that the previous head of the Service stopped the investigation, but he was also the one that instigated it. Said that people had spoken to him. Decided to pull out.'

'Lord Bairstow seems to have some connections. Serious connections,' said Susan.

'The agent that was being used,' said Hope, 'was Sylvia White. The same Sylvia White who is now lying in our morgue, after being dumped on the road.'

'What, she was actually working for Bairstow then? She was a double agent or something?' asked Macleod.

'No,' said Hope. 'Speaking to Anna Hunt, and she was very specific, Sylvia White was not working for anyone except the Service. She said she was an excellent agent. She got pulled off the case by the former head.'

'Sylvia White was also a secretary for Lord Bairstow,' said Ross. 'That came out. I saw her name in some of the investigation notes.'

'That was her cover,' said Hope. 'She was sent in to try to find out what was going on.'

'But she never got to,' said Macleod.

'But they never realised, Bairstow's lot, who she was, by the looks of it.'

'And neither,' said Perry, 'did those who wanted this all highlighted. They thought she was part of the conspiracy. If she was secretary to Bairstow, maybe they assumed she was involved. Were the other ones involved then? With this group?'

'Well, Sylvia White would have been involved with the group. That was what she was trying to get in to find out about. Where the money was going to. Whatever secret organisation Bairstow was running,' said Hope.

'Sean Devereaux was the accountant for Pear Holdings,' said Perry. 'That's why they've come for him. He must have been the one putting the money through. I'm not sure where MacTavish fits in yet. Was MacTavish running packages? Was MacTavish a gopher for them? Is he now still a gopher for them?'

'You don't think all three tie together, do they?' said Macleod. 'Some of it is about older things. Maybe some more modern. Maybe their evidence is sketchy. What they know is sketchy about Lord Bairstow.'

'You think they're wanting us to highlight everything again?'

'No, Susan,' said Macleod. 'I don't. I think this is different. This is so public it's almost like they're trying to force the issue. But you can't force the issue like that with the police; you have to go by certain routes; you can't just . . . well . . . we're not the Service; you can't just charge in. You have to gain evidence, you have to—'

'Oh, we haven't, though? What went on with Clarissa?' said Hope, looking at Macleod.

'That was different. We were working at where we were. That wasn't us bringing things to a court of law. If we're going to look at those sorts of killings and actually get the people at the top, we've got to amass evidence. We can't just walk in. If I'm honest, why not talk to Anna Hunt?'

'If the previous head was involved and complicit, why would they trust Anna?' said Hope. 'The Service isn't an easy bunch of people to trust, and I imagine in their history, some of these people who are trying to bring this other group to light, they would have, well, they may have been taken down by the Service at times, had their run-ins with them. Let's work out what we know, though.'

'Before that,' said Macleod, 'babies are being taken. This worries me. Why are these babies being taken? Two of them are linked to two of the people we have dead.'

'What about Lauren Starr, though, as well?' said Perry. 'I take it we're putting that down to Bairstow.'

'It's not easy to prove, is it?' said Susan.

'You can't prove it; that's the point,' said Perry. 'Everything around her, the information, has come from Lord Bairstow. She phoned in sick; his company said that. No record that she actually did it. No independent way of looking at that. Company called up, looking to see where MacTavish was. Nothing to say they didn't know. He was off getting a package for them, is what he told his sister. Company says, we know nothing about that. Do we know that for a fact? No, we only know it because they say it. I think Lauren Starr was used to try and cover up the first killing. So Bairstow's lot killed her. And set up that whole idea of an annoyed, angry boyfriend, a former partner. But it didn't sell. It's too much.'

'Agreed,' said Macleod. 'Far too much. And that's why the babies are worrying me. Bairstow's lot are covering up. But this other side, these people who want everything out in the light, they've come to us before and we've walked. We've solved certain things. We've saved Isbister's wife. She's now out in the open. We've highlighted what went on before.

'But they may force our hand. It's clear they want me, or us, to deal with the whole situation, and it's beyond us in one sense. We can't do what they want us to do, so maybe they're going to force it, make everybody take notice.'

'Sounds a bit far-fetched,' said Ross. 'Difficult for them to do. We're certainly getting close to home though, I think, with Bairstow.'

'Too close,' said Macleod. 'The reason I called you up and told you to be careful was because I was warned off. Jim came down. Our ACC told me, the chief constable had told him we had to be careful going after Bairstow without any evidence.'

'You think he's tapped people, up there? You think the Chief Constable's compromised?' said Perry.

'Jim's sound. Chief Constable, I've no evidence to say that he has been tapped at all. So, we have to assume that they are both kosher. But what this group will know is when people like the Chief Constable get rattled, they start asking questions and they start applying pressure. That's perfectly normal. That happens. It's a different thing to turn around and ask for people to stop being all over your back than it is to turn around and corrupt investigations,' said Macleod. 'I think Jim and the Chief Constable are well aware at the moment. They want this sorted, but have to be careful who they're dealing with. Bairstow may have friends up above, up above our own. Heads of the force.'

'So what do we do then?' said Susan.

'Right, well we go on what line of attack we have because Bairstow's not the one doing the killing. So, we have to go after that. We're going to struggle to get him for Lauren Starr.

But he didn't do the other three. So we need to find out who's doing that,' said Macleod.

'Well, we've seen the vehicle on CCTV. Jona has tyre tracks. But she can't match them up without a vehicle. So, we need to get the vehicle,' said Hope.

'Well we've got the cellophane-type material. Jona's onto that. We need to trace it,' said Susan. 'If we can trace it, we might trace the person. I've also gone through the rest of the CCTV from the recent incident. And the mainly red van which was seen moving ahead. It's seen leaving the other side, which is a change. Except it drives less than half a mile and it's gone. After that, I can't find it again.'

'It's shed the decals again,' said Perry. 'It's shed those decals. See, Susan was right with that all along. Those decals are important. We do need to go after them.'

'Right, then,' said Hope. 'That becomes one of our top priorities. How do we find it? How do we get that vehicle from the cellophane?'

'Well, Jona said,' continued Susan, 'that the cellophane material would need to be made somewhere. The type that it is, it's quickly removable, but it's massive. Normally, she said for something that size, you would use a permanent decal. It's not something you would make quickly then whip off again. Most of these decals that they stick on vans, are because you've got a business and you're going to have it for a long time. The quick ones are more the comedy-type ones. You know, monkey on board or sticking like a crack window over the back for a laugh. They're not what's going to be permanent. Things made for the size of the vehicle and for the amount in the vehicle. They're permanent, generally, according to Jona,' said Susan.

'Well then, we've got to see places that can actually do removable stuff. We've got to start searching for them. Get a list together,' ordered Hope. 'We can hunt them down. See if anybody's made anything that big.

'We'll get on to that then,' said Hope. 'See if we can find this van. Keep going through the CCTV as well. See if there's any chance of getting an identification on the drivers. Hopefully Jona might come up with something as well around that.'

'What about Bairstow?' said Ross.

'Keep it low level at the moment,' said Hope. 'Look, search, gather. We've got to be careful with him. Very careful.'

'Good,' said Macleod. 'Get to it. Keep me informed about what's going on.' The group pulled back their chairs and stood up from the table, but Macleod remained.

Hope could tell he wanted something. When the room had cleared and the office door was closed, Macleod stood up and sat on the edge of the table. Hope sat on her own desk.

'What's the matter?' she said.

He pulled out his phone, and held it up. 'Just been informed. Another baby missing. I haven't got details yet, but there's another one missing. I bet you there'll be a link to Sylvia White.'

'How? How could there be a link to Sylvia White? She's not a person—'

'How did they get a baby? Somebody's taken another baby,' said Macleod. 'Whatever they see about it, however they see it's linked. There's another one.

'Something's coming to a head, Hope,' said Macleod. 'I can feel it. We're getting kickback from Bairstow. We're going to get a kick from the other side, because we're not progressing fast enough. And we're going to get caught in the middle of this vice, both sides pushing in. We need to break one side. We need to get one side to stop.'

'Don't see what that's got to do with the babies.'

'I don't either,' said Macleod. 'I really don't, but you don't take innocence away like that for no reason. And the people that those babies are linked to are in our case. It's not a coincidence. It can't be. Too much of a coincidence not to be.'

'We'll get them,' said Hope. 'We'll get them.'

'I said I was out,' said Macleod. 'Told Anna I was out.'

'Well, Anna said you said that. Anna said that they're dealing you back in,' said Hope.

'So it would appear,' said Macleod.

Chapter 18

Macleod was frustrated as he drove over the Kessock Bridge on his way home for dinner with Jane. He felt like he was caught in the jaws of a press. On one side, he could get so little movement against Lord Bairstow, and it would be difficult to carry that through. If Bairstow pushed his connections up above, Macleod would need to make sure that everything was watertight. But the more they dug and hunted, the more he'd be aware that they were coming for him, and ranks would be closed.

On the other hand, the other jaw of the press, was this group who wanted Bairstow's lot put to the sword. Except they were putting people to the sword to get it done.

And yet in the middle were three babies. Three innocent children now missing. Macleod couldn't shake the feeling that they were involved in this. Somehow, in some way, they would be part of the deal. It was a funny thing that you could get into your head when people went after each other and there were killings, while both these sides were doing it to each other, it was somehow okay.

It wasn't with Gavin Isbister. He was an innocent in all of this. Simon Matthews was actually an innocent when you looked at it. But a lot of the other people who had died weren't.

They were involved. It was a dangerous cocktail. Two sides that had so much at stake.

Macleod had tried to steer his own ship away. He had tried to get his team away from looking into this. These types of things were best left to the Service. And as much as Macleod didn't like the Service, and he couldn't have worked within it, he recognised that they had a function. And things like this, which were so obviously wrong, but that needed stopped, required people who could work outside of the normal framework of the law.

Anna Hunt did a job that Macleod couldn't do. And at the moment, he wished she could just step in and do it. However, she couldn't, because she didn't know what was going on either.

It was getting overcast now, and the sky darkening, as Macleod turned off onto the Black Isle. He took the road through Munlochy, and then cut cross-country, before turning round towards the back roads that led to his house.

As he turned round towards the last one, he had to brake suddenly. There was a log across the road. Macleod froze for a moment. There'd been no wind. There'd been nothing to bring this down. He looked at the end of the log. No, this had been lifted from somewhere. He went to reverse, and suddenly a van spun in behind him, blocking his way out.

He opened the car door, tried to scramble out, to run away, but the van side door opened and he saw a couple of people in black hoods coming after him. At his age Macleod wasn't quick, and they were soon on top of him, hauling him down to the ground. He tried to fight back, but in truth, he was no match and soon they'd picked him up and were carrying him back into the van.

Macleod was thrown heavily inside, and he felt himself roll and hit the far wall. He then put his hands out but found them grabbed as a hood was suddenly put over his head. Darkness engulfed him. The van, however, didn't move. Macleod felt no motion. Instead, he was punched hard in the stomach, knocking the wind from him.

'Bairstow is guilty as hell. Get Bairstow,' said a voice. It was weird, because it wasn't like a normal human voice. It was synthesised. Somebody must have been speaking through a computer or some device to tell him.

'There's no evidence. We can't make a case,' said Macleod. He was punched hard again in the stomach and felt himself spit inside the hood. He tried to catch a breath.

'Bairstow. Bring down Bairstow.'

'We can't make evidence against Bairstow. We can't touch him. Talk to the Service. Talk to those who can operate in the dark.'

'Get Bairstow.'

'You couldn't get Bairstow,' said Macleod suddenly. 'You couldn't get him, and you don't have my rules. Don't have any of this, and you couldn't get him. What makes you think that when you amateurs, who can just do what you want, couldn't get him, that I can just waltz in as a police officer?'

Another punch hit him in the stomach. Macleod thought he was going to vomit. He was held down tight and rather than speak again, he took a moment to recover.

'DCI Macleod must bring Bairstow to justice. If there is no movement on Bairstow in three days, then the missing babies will be in trouble. This is to motivate you.'

Macleod could feel his body tense. His stomach suddenly pulled tight. Three days to get Bairstow. They could launch an operation for months and not get Bairstow. Bairstow was tightly packed away.

'Those are innocent kids. Innocents. You won't touch them.' Another punch hit Macleod in the stomach.

'DCI Macleod must be encouraged. Three days. We need to see movement against Bairstow in three days. Otherwise, babies will be highlighted in a bloody explosion.'

Even without a human voice, the words tore into Macleod.

'No. No, you won't. You won't do that. You won't touch them. They deserve none of this. I am hunting the group. I am hunting Bairstow. But we need time. You can't bring someone like Bairstow down in a couple of days.'

'You walked away, stopped investigating. You won't stop now. We will make sure.'

Macleod went to get himself off the floor of the van, but he was being held down. His stomach felt sore, muscles arguing against the punches they'd received.

'You don't understand. You really don't understand, do you? These people you're up against—'

'We found them for you. We gave them to you.'

'No, you didn't. You killed someone who was working on your side,' said Macleod.

'Macleod lies.'

'No, I don't,' said Macleod. 'Sylvia White, you don't even know who the hell Sylvia White was.' It was unlike Macleod to swear. But he wasn't sure he was going to get back out of this van, so he was going to tell them.

'Sylvia White worked for the Service. Sylvia White was infiltrating. Sylvia White—'

'Sylvia White was a secretary of Bairstow's. Worked with Bairstow. We understood the connection to Circle and

147

connection to the group. Sylvia White is dead because of her connection.'

'Sylvia White was undercover,' said Macleod.

There was a quiet suddenly, as if people in the van were looking at each other. Maybe they were. Macleod couldn't tell. His face was sweating. It was claustrophobic inside the bag that had been put over his head, warm and sweaty.

'It does not matter,' said the voice suddenly. 'What matters is Macleod shows movement against Bairstow. So, three days.'

Macleod lay there. This was crazy. How was this going to work? How did they think in three days you just jumped up and found evidence and did things? Where did that come from? But he wasn't arguing with sane people. Far from it.

'Three days,' said the voice. 'Do you understand?'

Macleod wasn't engaging with them. There was no way he was engaging with them. He said nothing. The next thing he knew, he was punched hard again in the stomach.

'Answer! Three days, or the children die!'

Macleod refused to say anything until he was punched again. 'You will tell us, you understand.'

The next punch came on his chin. Macleod felt his head fly back and hit the van floor. He was pulled forward again. 'Tell us you understand!'

'I understand,' said Macleod. 'I get it. But you, you're wrong. You don't understand it. You haven't got a clue. I haven't got the power to do that.'

Macleod felt his arms and legs being lifted. For a moment, he felt himself being swung quickly back and forward. And then his limbs were let go and he sailed out of the van.

He hit the ground hard, rolling over and over. Hearing an engine fire up, he thought the van must be pulling away. He tried to get to his feet, but he was stumbling. His hands went up to the hood that was over him. But it was tight, and he couldn't lift it off.

It didn't seem to move, as if there was some sort of catch put on it. He could stand up and walk, but where was he walking? He could walk into anything. Macleod was angry, frustrated, but he sat down on his bottom. There was no point charging about, no point running here and there. It was times like this that you had to be calm.

It was easier said than done. He reached down and found his phone in his trouser pocket. He picked it up and pressed the on switch at the side. Of course, he couldn't see the screen. He knew it would be on, but what could he do with it without being able to see it?

He sat for a moment. Then he remembered. It was three months ago, wasn't it? Ross had tried to explain to him how to use voice activation on the phone. There was a button on the side that you pressed. That was the first thing you did. He ran his hands around the phone and found the unfamiliar button on the left-hand side. He pressed it.

'Call Jane,' he said, but nothing came back. 'Call Jane.' Again, there was nothing. 'I said call Jane! My partner! Would you call Jane?'

He tried to take deep breaths, because he was getting angry. *What did Ross say? Press the button on the side. Yes, I've done that. 'It'll allow you to speak'.*

I'm speaking. It's doing nothing, Ross, thought Macleod. *'Make sure you unlock the phone first.'*

'Stupid, you clown!' he said to himself. He pressed the button on the side again. 'Unlock phone.'

'Phone unlocked,' said a voice.

149

'Phone Jane.'

'Calling Jane,' came the reply. He couldn't hear much, though, but he put the phone up to his ear. And then heard a ringing tone.

'Seoras, what's up? You not coming for dinner?'

'Jane, I need you to stay calm. When I tell you the next bit, I want you to stay calm. Okay?'

'What?' said Jane suddenly.

'I'm down the road from our house. I'll need you to leave the house and come down the road. Bring a knife or some scissors or something. Something sharp. Okay? You'll see a log across the road. You'll see my car. I'm somewhere near it.'

'What do you mean, you're somewhere near it?'

'I've been attacked. And I've got a hood over my head. I can't get it off.'

'What? You've been attacked. I'll call the station. I'll—'

'No,' said Macleod. 'It's fine. I need you to do this. Bring some scissors. Bring a knife. You might have to cut the hood open that's over my head.'

'I'm coming,' she said. 'I'm coming.'

'Keep the phone with you. Jane?'

But Jane was gone. Macleod put the phone down, unaware if he'd cancelled the call or what else was happening on the screen. Instead, he sat there, and for several minutes, was almost serene.

He couldn't look anywhere; he couldn't stare, but he could hear the birds. And after what had just happened, he was thankful.

'Seoras! Dear God, Seoras!' He heard her come running towards him.

'I'm fine. I'm okay,' he said. He heard her drop to her knees beside him, throw her arms around him, and squeeze.

His stomach hurt like hell when she did it, but he didn't have the heart to tell her to get off. When she broke off, he said, 'You need to get the hood off me.'

'It's got a plastic tie fixing it,' she said. 'Hang on. Don't move.'

For thirty seconds, he didn't move and then he heard a click as something came away. The bag was pulled off over the top of his head.

His face was grabbed, and Jane planted a kiss on his lips and then on his forehead.

'Are you okay? Hey, are you all right?'

'Help me up,' he said. He stood up and she could see him hunched slightly.

'What's wrong?' she said.

'Punched me in the stomach several times. It's okay, but it's sore.'

'You also got one to your chin.'

'Took a punch there, too. Flung me out of the van. Let's get up to the house. We need to get somebody to come and help move that log.'

'Don't forget your phone,' she said, bending down and picking it up for him. 'What's all this about?' asked Jane.

'It's just work,' said Macleod. 'It's not something for you.'

'I'm calling Hope when we get in,' said Jane. 'You're telling somebody about this.'

'Oh, believe me,' said Macleod. 'I'm going to have to tell everyone about this one.'

Chapter 19

'**A**nd you say he's all right?'

'He's okay. A little sore around the ribs and the stomach. I think he took a couple of punches,' said Ross. 'Anyway, the rest of us need to get our heads down and keep going. Just be careful out there, Perry.'

'Of course,' said Perry, closing down the call.

He looked at the phone and saw a list of addresses had arrived via email.

'What's the matter?' asked Susan.

'The big boss got jumped last night getting back to his house, apparently. They've said the three babies that have been taken, they're going to die in some sort of explosion unless we find out more about Bairstow.'

'Really?' Susan turned away and looked out of the car window. 'Is he okay?' she asked.

'Yes, apparently he's fine. Sore and tender, but it kind of puts the pressure on, doesn't it? Especially for Hope. I mean, she's carrying one of her own. Can't be easy.'

'No, I'm sure it can't be.'

Perry took off round Inverness and began driving to the few shops that did decals. Along with Susan, they questioned the owners. Most sold decals that were small. Nothing big and very few had the ability to make their own. That was the key, wasn't it? How to fit a car with decals.

Ross had looked up if there were any standard ones that you could put on a van like this, but there were none of that size. It had to be a custom job. And so far, most of the shops in Inverness didn't do a custom version. They continued to drive round and then expanded out, making their way up north towards Tain before then routing back south again. As they drove into their last shop just south of Inverness, Perry was shaking his head.

'It's a great bit of work you've done,' he said to Susan, 'but it doesn't feel like this is going to come up with something.'

'It will. You had to have that made somewhere,' said Susan. 'You wouldn't just make it off your own bat. Ross would have come up with suppliers otherwise. People who would have that type of machine for it.'

'I suppose,' said Perry. 'Anyway, let's get this one done. Then we'll head back.'

The pair strode into what was quite a small shop and Perry saw the car decals on the side, all hanging in their little plastic pouches from a stand.

'It's not the right sort. Look at it.'

'Doesn't matter,' said Susan; 'let's see what we've got.'

A middle-aged woman stood behind a till and Susan approached her.

'Hi, we're looking for car decals.'

'That's the rack over there,' said the woman.

'No, what we're looking for is ones that are big enough to cover a van, like a large stripe that went all the way across a van, covering fifty, sixty, seventy percent of it.'

'You will not find them in this shop,' said the woman. 'That's a big job. I'm trying to think where else you would get them. What sort of things are you looking for exactly because I didn't think they did permanent ones of that size? You would just paint the van.'

Perry turned and nodded at Susan. So, Susan continued with the woman, pulling out a sample of the decal she'd recovered from the bin lorry. 'This is the type of thing it's made of,' she said, and handed it over to the woman.

'Ah, right,' said the woman. 'Now, this is different. This is non-permanent vinyl. You use that for indoor and temporary decals, but you don't use that on cars. There are places that will do that. But you need to be looking for someone that's selling custom indoor decal, not car places. This isn't the sort of material you would use for a car or a van or anything like that.'

'Why?'

'It's not permanent, is it? You could pull it back off quickly but more than that, it would come off. You put a decal on the car and you want it to last a year, two years, whatever,' said the woman. 'This stuff you'd be lucky if this stuff lasted a couple of weeks by the time the rain and the wind and the cold got to it.'

'So, you're telling me we should look for something else, then? A different sort of shop?'

'Interior decals. Look around that. Somebody there might be able to do it. It's big though. If you're talking about a van, you'll need a reasonable size machine for that. Either that or it'll have to be well designed, but even then, yeah, you need a big one.'

'Okay,' said Susan. 'Thank you for that. Very helpful.' When they exited the shop, Susan turned to Perry. 'Looking in the wrong place all day today.'

'Well, let's call Ross, see if he can come up with any more.'

Perry spoke to Ross on the phone, and while Susan and Perry grabbed a coffee, Ross went back onto the internet before sending through a new list. He called shortly afterwards to Perry.

'There are one or two places in Inverness. You can get those done tonight,' said Ross. 'But there's also one in Pitlochry. Given the previous cases . . .'

'Given the previous cases,' said Perry, 'it's well worth a look. We'll get down there tonight. We'll wrap up these two in Inverness and then head south.'

'Pitlochry,' said Susan, when Perry closed the call down.

'There's a shop in Pitlochry. There's two in Inverness. We'll check through quickly but then we're heading down the road.'

They quickly made their way to the Inverness shops and were told they did nothing that size and certainly didn't have the machinery to produce something that large. By now it was just getting after six o'clock and so they drove towards Pitlochry as the evening light was diminishing. By the time they arrived, it was almost dark and Susan directed Perry as he drove, pointing out where the shop was.

'Happy Home,' said Perry, reading the sign above the shop. 'Does it really look like a place that's going to do a car decal?'

'That's the point, Perry, though, isn't it?' said Susan. 'It's not about whether it does car decals. It's the wrong type of material for a car decal, but it suits their purpose. You put it on, you drive past the traffic camera, you pull in somewhere, and you can peel it off quick and easy. Turn the van into something else.'

Perry walked up to the window of the shop and looked in.

'This is all, like, cushions and stuff like that.'

'No,' said Susan, peering past him. 'Look, over there. Those are decals.'

'They're quite small, though, aren't they?'

'That one isn't. Look at the size of that one on the wall.'

There was a comic cat on the wall, and it was holding a sign saying, 'Custom decal for you.' Susan looked up at Perry and smiled.

'See? That's the sort of thing we're looking for. That's big. I mean, that's nearly the height of a van. This place must be able to do the image.'

'It's not open, though, is it?' said Perry. 'We'll catch them in the morning, I think.'

'We could try them now. Find the owner.'

'Okay,' said Perry and they retreated back to their laptops. Eventually, they found a number for the shop and stood outside it, awaiting an answer for their call. Perry could hear the phone inside.

'What about the owners?' asked Perry.

'Let's see where it's registered to, if we can,' said Susan. It took them a while, but eventually they got a phone number for the owner. Their name was registered with Companies House but they were also in the phone book.

Perry called but there was no answer. He left a message on the machine before driving round. On arrival, they found the house was dark.

'Not in then,' said Susan.

'Let's check the neighbours,' said Perry. After talking to the neighbours, they found that the woman who owned the shop was away on holiday. She wouldn't be back for a couple of weeks. The shop was still opening, but the neighbours didn't know the staff who worked for the owner. Perry decided they'd call it a night because it was getting close to ten o'clock.

'We better find somewhere,' said Perry. 'I'm also starving.'

'Not surprised. We haven't eaten any tea yet,' said Susan. They picked up a hotel on the edge of Pitlochry and went straight down to dinner. The hotel sat beside a small loch, and they took up a seat at a window, allowing them a view over the loch. There were pretty lights all the way round it, and Susan looked at them dreamily.

'This is nice, isn't it?' she said, while they were waiting for their food.

Perry smiled. 'It is,' he said. 'I'll get drinks from the bar. Do you want something?'

She nodded, and he came back with a couple of cokes to await his meal.

'What was Glasgow like?' asked Susan.

'Excuse me?' said Perry.

'What was Glasgow like?'

'Glasgow?' said Perry. 'Well, I worked for Macleod for a while. He's different now than he was then. To be honest, he was, I always thought, a little bitter. Still clever. Very astute. But he's changed since he came up here. I think Jane's done a lot for him. Different man to what I used to know. Very religious, very conservative, back then. Not the same now. Seems happier. Seems more settled, more balanced.'

'Is there anything else about Glasgow?'

'What do you mean?' asked Perry.

'Anything else you did down there? Anybody else?'

'I played in the football leagues. Could move in those days,' said Perry. 'I feel I don't move the same as I used to.'

'What I meant was,' said Susan, 'did you not have any women

on the go?'

Perry stopped for a moment. 'Women on the go?' said Perry. 'You make me sound like some sort of gigolo or hot stud. No, I didn't have women on the go.'

'All that time down there and what? Nobody special?'

'Do you have anybody special up here?'

Susan looked away for a moment. 'No,' she said. 'I really wasn't—'

'I know all the rumours, I know what they say about you, and what you did when you were in uniform.' Susan blushed. 'Doesn't bother me,' said Perry. 'We all go through times. We've all been there, loved and lost and whatever.'

'Have you really? Who?'

Perry's phone rang. He looked across at Susan. 'Must be important, this time of night,' he said. He picked up the phone feeling relieved. 'Do you mind if I talk here?' Susan shook her head. Perry pressed down to answer the call without really looking at the phone.

'Hello, Perry,' said a voice on the other end. It was Tanya.

'Oh, hello,' said Perry.

'Just wondering where you were,' said Tanya. 'Wondering if you wanted a late nightcap or something.'

'Out of town, actually,' said Perry. 'Off on the case. So, no. Are you just leaving now?'

'Yes,' said Tanya.

'Macleod shouldn't be working you that late,' said Perry.

'Just catching things up. I thought I might catch you for a nightcap, but you weren't here, so I thought I'd better ring.'

'No, Susan and I have got tasked down the A9. We're in Pitlochry for the night.'

'Pitlochry for the night?'

'Yes,' said Perry. 'Stuck down here. Got to go to a shop in the morning.'

'All right. Just the two of you?'

'Well, we normally investigate as a pair,' said Perry. He looked over at Susan—she seemed keen to know who he was on the phone to. 'Best let you go then, I guess. Maybe another night.'

'Maybe,' said Perry. 'See how this case goes.' He closed the call down.

'Who was that, calling at this time of night?' asked Susan. Perry could see she already had the answer.

'Tanya,' said Perry. He looked at Susan and thought he saw a little bit of fire behind her eyes. 'What's she want at this time of night?'

'Apparently, she wanted to know if I wanted to go for a drink.'

'All right. She was in Glasgow with you, wasn't she? I was talking about Glasgow and you never mentioned her. You knew her well?'

'Oh, look,' said Perry. 'Here's the food.' He leaned back as the waitress slid a plate of beef in front of him. 'Best we eat up, get to bed. Got an early start in the morning,' said Perry.

Susan gave him a stare, which, while not unkind, let him know she understood that there was more to Tanya than just a colleague. Perry finished his food quickly and after dropping Susan off at her room, he made his way into his own.

He took off his shirt and tie, got changed into his pyjama bottoms, and then stood in the bathroom, looking at himself before the bathroom mirror. Perry turned sideways, tapped his belly, and then turned the other way, tapping it again. He raised his arms, flexing his muscles as best he could.

'How on earth, Perry boy, did you end up like this? Two of them, two of them wanting this.'

He laughed at himself for a moment. Then he shook his head. Why two at once? Tanya would be the obvious choice. 'My age, we know we get on,' he said to himself. 'But Susan is, Susan's something else, again.' He switched off the bathroom light and went to his bed.

He was about to lie down and then went and grabbed a small pair of earphones. He plugged them in and switched on the music from his phone. Perry knew if he didn't, his mind would reel around the two women, trying to work out what was the right thing to do. In truth, he wasn't sure there was a right or a wrong.

Chapter 20

You're looking well this morning,' said Susan as Perry approached at breakfast. *Had she done her hair?* It wasn't in a ponytail at the moment, it was hanging loose. She had jeans on and a tight t-shirt. Her leather jacket was currently sitting over the back of her chair.

'Morning,' said Perry. 'I'm feeling okay today. Let's get eating and get out. Nine o'clock the shop opened, wasn't it?'

'Yes,' said Susan. 'Probably plenty of time.'

'Well, they might be there by about half eight, getting ready to open. I think we should get there and see who works there.'

'We'll just go in and ask them,' said Susan.

'Not so sure,' said Perry. He stood up and went over to the buffet the hotel had laid out, picking up some croissants, a couple of bits of bacon on the side of his plate and some scrambled egg. As he did so, Susan joined him.

'No more mysterious callers?' she said.

'No,' said Perry. He brought the plate back to the table, sat down, eating, and Susan sat opposite, a smile on her face.

'You think this will work?' she said to Perry.

'Well, let's hope it's going to work. We've got those babies to think of. I can't believe they actually took the boss and jumped him. It's a bit of a change. It seems like they're prompting us, and then suddenly it's not a prompt anymore. Now, it's a threat. We're not the people to deal with this,' said Perry. 'You think back on it. Emmett was shot at. Hope had to jump on board a boat and then get back off. And I heard that Clarissa's trip away was quite rough. This is not what we want to be doing. We want to be out of this. Gone.'

'Doesn't look like they want to let us go, though.'

'No, it doesn't. But this is the world of that Kirsten. I mean, she's a grand lass,' said Perry. 'But man, she's brutal. Fast. Agile.'

'I thought you guys liked that sort of woman.'

'What?' said Perry. 'A woman that could kill with her own hands.'

'What type of a woman do you like, then?' asked Susan.

'I'm easily pleased,' said Perry.

'Rubbish. No, you're not.'

No, I'm not, thought Perry. Susan dipped her head to eat from her plate. Perry took the chance to look at her. *Not easily pleased at all.* He looked away as she looked back up.

'Come on,' he said, 'we best get eating; get out to this shop.'

By half-past eight, Perry and Susan were sitting in the car just down from the shop. Pitlochry's main street was already busy. Not quite like Inverness, first thing on a Monday morning, but it definitely was busy. People were getting ready for the day, the school run passing through, workers approaching the shops. As they sat there, Susan spotted some women coming to work at the shop. Two of them stopped outside it and stood waiting until a third one arrived.

'That's them,' said Susan, going to get out of the car.

Perry put his hand across. 'No,' he said. 'Don't!'

'Don't? What do you mean, "don't?"'

162

Perry reached down and took a camera out of the glove box compartment. He turned and aimed it, photographing the women before they went in.

'What did you do that for?' asked Susan. 'I was just going to talk to them.'

'Just a thought,' said Perry. 'Remember that Emmett's been down here before with Sabine. I just want to check any of the people in this shop aren't people they know. We could be walking into something, after all. This is where it all started. This is where Isbister was killed. Simon Matthews, too. The double grave. Probably wise that we check with those who've been before.'

Perry grabbed his phone.

'This is Emmett. Hello, Perry.'

'Emmett, I'm down in Pitlochry,' said Perry. He could hear a shuffling on the phone.

'Okay,' said Emmett. 'How can I help you?'

'Well, thing is, I'm investigating a shop. Happy Home. You heard of it?'

'No. Unaware of it.'

'Okay. Well, I took a photograph of three women who work there, and I thought I would send it up to you, see if you recognise anyone from your time down here on that investigation.'

'Send it up, then. I'll have a look. Got Sabine here, too. She can check, too.'

'With the boss getting jumped last night,' said Perry, 'I thought it wise if I know who I'm talking to.'

'Absolutely,' said Emmett. 'Send me the photos. I'll ring you back in a minute.'

Perry closed the call, sent the photographs through the

163

internet, and then waited. He could see Susan was itching to go in. He understood this was her idea. She was the one who had traced down the decals. She was the one who, ultimately, he would turn round and say well done to, if anything came from this. But Perry wanted to be cautious.

'He's taking his time, isn't he?' said Susan.

'It's only been two minutes,' said Perry as his phone vibrated. He answered it.

'Hello, Emmett. What have you got for us?'

'Sabine agrees with me,' said Emmett. 'Emma Matthews is there.'

'Emma Matthews? Simon Matthews' daughter?'

'Yes, that's Emma Matthews. We met her once. She was there with his wife, in Pitlochry, I didn't realise she actually lived there.'

'Which one was she?'

'The middle one, the one with the key.'

'She must be looking after the shop while the actual owner is away. That's interesting.'

'You need to watch yourself,' said Emmett. 'If she's there, and tied in, you don't know which side she's batting for. She may be part of this group that's trying to highlight everything.'

'Well, the connection came from their van. Susan's found a decal on the van, and it's led us here.'

'I would consult Hope before you do anything else,' said Emmett.

'Oh, well, thank you,' said Perry. He closed the call down and set his phone up in the middle of the car. He rang Hope with a video call.

'What's up, Perry?' asked Hope. She looked flustered on the video screen. It was her office, but she wasn't dressed like she was in the office. Hope was very casual normally. But currently she was wearing a jumper. That wasn't Hope. It was a smart blouse or a t-shirt. This was a sloppy jumper.

'You okay?' asked Perry.

'I'm fine, Perry,' she said. But she wasn't convincing.

'I take it the old man's all right.'

'Seoras is okay. He's a bit roughed up. He's more worried about the kids. These babies. I am too.'

'Listen. Good news,' said Perry. 'We followed Susan's decal off the van. We're now down in Pitlochry.'

'Pitlochry? But that's where—'

'That's where it all started,' said Perry. 'We're outside a shop that we think produces the decal. I got hold of Emmett because I photographed the women who were opening up the shop this morning. Emmett's identified one of them as Emma Matthews.

'Simon Matthews' daughter?'

'Exactly,' said Perry. 'We're trying to work out what we should do now.'

'We should go in,' said Susan. 'We need to make an approach and find out what's going on and get hold of these babies.'

'What do you think, Perry?' asked Hope.

'I disagree,' said Perry. 'We've got a bit of time. We need to find out where these babies are. I would say we watch her for a bit. If she's involved, in that sense, she'll make calls or she'll go somewhere.'

'True,' said Hope, 'but if we get nothing from her, we've wasted a day. We could go in and be heavy-handed, pull her in.'

'They won't say anything, though,' said Perry. 'These people are fanatics. They're nuts, blind to anything outside their cause.

165

Hope, they took out a Service agent because they didn't follow their facts, didn't realise they don't know all that's going on. You pull her in, I don't think she'll say a word,' said Perry. 'Unless you're going to get somebody like Kirsten to come and deal with her and extract that information.'

'Can't do,' said Hope, 'even if I wanted to. Seoras says we need to make things stick at the moment with Lord Bairstow.'

'Well, I get where he's coming from with that, but there may come a time when—'

'There may do. I'm coming down,' said Hope. 'She's our best bet at the moment, so I'm going to come down. If we're interrogating her, I want to be there.'

'I can handle it,' said Perry.

'I know,' said Hope, 'but I want to be there.'

'She doesn't know us yet, does she?' asked Susan.

'No,' said Perry.

'Right then,' said Susan. 'I will not interfere, but I'm going to go inside.'

'Okay. For what purpose?' asked Perry.

'To see if she's going anywhere, to see what's happening. The boss of the shop isn't there. She came in with the keys. Is she staying put? Because if she's going to have anything to do with these babies, she's going to have to hand keys over. Somebody else is going to have to look after the place. I'll go in and see if I can hear anything. Early morning conversation.'

'Is the shop open yet?' asked Perry.

'No,' said Susan. 'It will be in fifteen minutes.'

'Right,' said Hope. 'Do that, but make sure you don't get clocked. I'm on my way, okay?'

Perry closed down the call and Susan went to get out of the car.

166

'Where are you going? Fifteen minutes.'

'I'll come in from a different angle, a different place. Not from the car here.'

Susan went to go, but Perry grabbed her hand. 'Be careful.'

'I am careful.'

Perry squeezed her hand. 'Remember what happened to the boss. I don't want it to happen to you.'

Susan gave a nod and left. Perry saw her disappear into the shop approximately fifteen minutes later, after it had just opened. She was in there for a good twenty minutes, before she suddenly walked out and got into the car.

'What's the matter? You look, well, excited,' said Perry.

'She handed the keys over. She handed the keys over and she was talking to one of the other women, telling her what to do. About what's happening for the next couple of days?'

'Really?' said Perry. 'That's good.' He sat back in the seat. 'Just got to wait for her to leave, then.'

'She'll walk out of here, though,' said Susan. 'Maybe I should follow her then when she comes out.'

'No,' said Perry. 'I'll follow her. She doesn't know me yet. She knows you. You stay in the car. I'll see where she goes. If she gets in a car herself, you can pick me up.'

'Okay,' said Susan. 'Don't get too close.'

Perry got out and disappeared over to a shop. From inside of it, he could watch the front door of Happy Home. When he saw Emma Matthews leave, he exited the shop he was in and tailed her at a distance. She walked down a few streets before getting into a car. Perry picked up his phone and continued to walk. Susan drove past, picking him up, and then speeding up quickly to the end of the street to see Emma Matthews take a right.

Susan stuck close behind her, but with enough cars between them. Emma Matthews returned to her house. She came back out with a bag, throwing it into the boot before getting back in her car. She drove out, leaving Pitlochry, and as she did so, Perry picked up the phone, calling Hope.

'I'm in the car at the moment. Can't do video,' said Hope.

'You might want to put a delay on your travels,' said Perry. 'Emma Matthews has handed keys over for the shop. She's just picked up a bag, and we're now leaving Pitlochry.'

'And where's she going?'

'Hang on,' said Perry. Perry sat back, watching Emma Matthews' car approach the A9. It took a right.

'Heading up the A9,' said Perry. 'Possibly up towards Inverness.'

'Tail her,' said Hope. 'Tail her and don't lose her. This is our chance. And Susan. Good work, really good work.'

Perry closed down the call and turned to see a smiling Susan. She looked at him and gave him a brief smile. 'Knew it would come through,' she said. 'I knew it.'

'I knew you would too,' said Perry. He sat back in the seat, anticipating the drive ahead. But part of him was also wondering where they were going to end up. Today could be the day to find the kids. Perry hoped they would be in time.

Chapter 21

Hope McGrath pulled back into the station car park. Once she'd stopped the car, she let out a puff, even though it was barely ten in the morning. She was still feeling the pace. That morning had been another one of spending half an hour in the bathroom before she'd been able to get going. It didn't help that John was worried.

He said to her she should pull back, let somebody else carry the caseload at the moment. But Hope couldn't do that, could she? Macleod had just been attacked, after all. She couldn't dump it on him to suddenly step in. And besides, if he thought that was the case, he'd have stepped in by now. Instead, he wanted her to continue to run the investigation while he floated above.

There were bigger things than just the investigation going on. Matters that needed a separate handle. Someone to keep watch while Hope got into the nitty gritty of what was happening in this particular case. As she trudged up the stairs of the police station, she continued up past the floor of her office and to the top floor where Macleod's was located.

As she approached, she saw Tanya, head down, typing into a computer. But as Hope went to go past, there was an abrupt voice.

'Detective Inspector, I'm afraid that the DCI is busy at the moment.'

'He'll need to know about this,' said Hope, and continued towards the door.

She was amazed at how quick Tanya could move. The woman was right on her heels by the time Hope had reached the door. 'I said he's busy at the moment.'

'You are aware,' said Hope, 'of who I am. And you're aware that we're in the middle of quite a busy case.'

'Yes,' said Tanya. 'But the DCI is busy at the moment.'

'You don't normally block me from going in.'

'No, but the DCI isn't normally busy for you. At the moment, he is.'

'I really need to see him at the moment,' said Hope.

Tanya slipped round the back of her, and then appeared in front of her, blocking her path to the door. 'If you'll kindly wait here, I'll just see if he's available for you.'

Hope went to shout at the woman, but instead, she took a deep breath, as Tanya knocked crisply on the door, and then popped inside the office.

'DI McGrath is here to see you. Is it convenient?'

'Tell her to come on in,' said Macleod. Tanya turned round and opened the door fully, and as Hope walked past, said, 'Can I get you a coffee?'

'No. No, thank you.'

Tanya calmly left the room, closing the door behind her, and Hope saw why Tanya had blocked her arrival. The Assistant Chief Constable, Jim, was sitting opposite Macleod at his desk.

'Come on in, Hope. Grab a seat,' said Macleod. 'Jim just popped in to see me.'

'I've been asked again to keep your lot out of the affairs of

Bairstow.'

'But we're not in the affairs of Bairstow at the moment,' said Hope. 'We checked, we went through what we had. There's nothing else we can particularly do at the moment. DS Ross, I don't believe, is chasing anything.'

'No, he's not,' said Macleod. 'I just called him.'

'I'm not happy about this,' said Jim. 'You should be entitled to investigate who you want, as and when you want. But the Chief Constable was insistent.'

'What's the deal?' said Macleod. 'If we're not investigating, who is and who's going into that detail.'

'Specifically,' said Jim, 'Lord Bairstow has complained about being under surveillance.'

Hope looked at Macleod for a moment, then back to Jim. 'He's not under surveillance from us.'

'As far as I'm aware, we're not surveilling anyone,' said Macleod.

'Well, that's not strictly true,' said Hope. 'As of half an hour ago, we're currently tailing Emma Matthews.'

'Emma Matthews?' said Macleod. 'Where?'

'It goes back to the decal on the van that the bodies were being dumped out of. The team traced the type of decal and came up with a shop in Pitlochry. They haven't confirmed it came from there, but Emma Matthews is working in that shop. The owner is away, and she is looking after the shop, except she's handed the keys over to someone else and is now, currently, driving up the A9.'

'So, who's tailing her?' asked Macleod.

'Perry and Susan.'

Macleod took a moment to let that information bed in. 'So,' he said, 'she may be involved with this. She would have a lot

171

of the background certainly. Her mother, Mrs Matthews, I believe, told Emmett that her husband Simon didn't talk about the case. Maybe he did. Remember, he had notes that were pulled,' said Macleod. 'Either way, there's a good chance she would know all the detail. Simon Matthews was one of the first people to accuse and to point out a lot of the issues.'

'Doesn't explain who's tailing Lord Bairstow,' said Jim.

'Kirsten,' said Hope, looking over at Macleod.

'Kirsten?' said Jim.

'Kirsten Stewart,' said Macleod to Jim. 'Keeping an eye on everybody at the moment.'

'Is she tailing Lord Bairstow?' asked Jim.

'Not that I'm aware of,' said Macleod. 'And also, she wouldn't be seen, not by somebody of Bairstow's calibre.'

'Service then?' asked Hope.

'No,' said Macleod. 'That would be similar. If Anna Hunt was having the Service tail Bairstow, she'd be doing it subtly. I know she wants to investigate him. She won't put an obvious tail on him. That would bring his attention and question her loyalty.'

'Her loyalty?' said Jim.

'The Service, at times, has been at the whim of certain people,' said Macleod. 'I don't understand it fully. But when I last spoke to Anna Hunt, she said that her previous colleague, who ran the Service, would have been a lot more flexible with approaches by people in higher power. Anna's not like that.'

'Are you sure?' asked Jim.

'Very,' said Macleod.

'Maybe it's the other group,' said Hope. 'Maybe they're watching Bairstow.'

'But why?' said Jim.

'Maybe they're going to attack him,' said Hope.

'Again, why?' said Jim. 'You've just taken the babies hostage. Why would you attack him? You're calling him out. You're trying to make sure that he's held up to public account, or at least investigated. Why bother grabbing Macleod here?'

'They want the whole backstory revealed,' said Macleod. 'That's what this is about. So, take the babies, hold them hostage. Press will be all over it. Road victims causing traffic to be stopped. Highlighted to everyone. If they can highlight Bairstow at the same time,' said Macleod, 'then maybe . . .'

'But exactly what are they doing? Are they going to attack him?' asked Jim.

'No,' said Macleod. 'Before, they hived off bits and pieces off of the group. They had a line of attack. Basically killed everyone they knew of and then got stuck. They're now trying to investigate from a different angle. If they get rid of Bairstow, where do they go? If they get rid of Bairstow, how do they get us to investigate? On the other hand, how do they get from him what he knows? It makes no sense for them to attack Bairstow.'

'Maybe they've sent more agencies in. Maybe they got the press onto him,' said Hope.

'It's a flawed plan though,' says Jim. 'It's not going to work, is it? Bairstow will never talk.'

'I agree,' said Hope. 'They're not very good at coming forward. When Clarissa found a contact down in Oxford, he didn't speak. He told her a way for her to investigate, but he didn't come out. He tried to hide away. He tried to run. But they came for him. And they came for him on the slightest whim. They didn't know he'd broken contact. He didn't know that they'd betrayed him, in one sense.'

'So,' said Jim, 'we're saying that they don't really know what they're doing. And it's a flawed plan.'

'Just because it's flawed doesn't mean it's not happening,' said Macleod. 'That's something to bear in mind.'

'They will not tell us where the babies are being held, will they?' said Hope. 'That's key. They'll force us to arrest Bairstow or make something out of him. But that'll mean his lawyers will come in. We'll not be able to make anything stick. We'll not be able to—'

'No,' said Macleod. 'We haven't got the evidence. And the way the Chief Constable is at the moment, I don't think we're going to get backup either to hold Bairstow indefinitely. The way Bairstow needs to be resolved is—'

'With the Service,' said Jim. 'They're the ones who could solve him. They're the ones who could take him out.'

Macleod shook his head. 'If they go ahead and kill these babies, it'll be tagged to Bairstow. Somehow, someway, he'll be tagged to it. I don't know how yet.'

'When do we make a move on Emma Matthews?' asked Hope. 'We could haul her in. We could—' She stopped for a moment, looked at Jim, and then looked at Macleod. 'Kirsten,' she said.

'What do you mean Kirsten?' asked Jim.

'Because Kirsten's ex-Service, Kirsten could bring Emma Matthews in, and she would have means and methods of trying to make her talk,' said Hope.

'But that would mean—-' started Jim.

'It would mean that any evidence coming from that interview would not be admissible. It could, however, save our babies. But what it wouldn't do is achieve the end of bringing Bairstow to justice,' said Macleod.

'It's a ruddy mess,' said Jim. 'So, what's our plan of attack?'

'We've got Emma Matthews. That's where we go,' said Macleod. 'We let her run at the moment. If we need to, we'll pull her in once the time gets closer.'

'The babies' safety is paramount here,' said Jim.

'I agree,' said Macleod. 'But I don't think we'll actually get them back safe and sound if we move now. Two reasons. One, they'd have a chance to move them from wherever they are if they realise that Emma's gone out of the picture too quick. And two, I don't think she'll speak quickly. I think bringing her in and coercing her to talk is the last effort. And frankly, it's not police work.'

'No,' said Jim. 'It just means it begins again. Even if you save them, you just go on to the next one. And they keep building.'

'Yes,' said Macleod. 'They keep building, and it gets worse.'

'I'll deflect when I can from above,' said Jim. 'Keep me in the loop. Good luck.' He stood up, gave Hope a nod, and left the room.

'So that's our game plan? You're not going to bring Kirsten in.'

'Kirsten's been in all along,' said Macleod. 'It's not safe right out there at the moment.'

'They attacked you. She wasn't doing a good job at that point.'

'They're not going to despatch me. They're trying to prompt me into exposing Bairstow. I'm not at risk like that. Sure, I've got a tender stomach, bruising, but they won't kill me. At least not the side that's trying to bring everything to light. Bairstow's lot, maybe,' said Macleod. 'Same with yourself.'

'So, what do we do?' said Hope.

'What we said. Follow Emma Matthews. If it gets too tight

for time, we'll bring her in. We'll see if we can get her to talk. And then we rescue the kids. But if we do it that way and we don't end up with any evidence, we are going to go back into the same loop next time. I mean, they'll just pull in another thread that leads up to this group.'

'Well, let's hope that Perry and Susan come through.'

'Whether or not they do is irrelevant,' said Macleod, 'in the grander scheme. Yes, it's very relevant to those three lives that we're trying to save, but not in the grander scheme. In the grander scheme, once this is done, we have to stop it. We have to go on the offensive.'

Hope looked at him. 'In what way?'

'One thing at a time,' said Macleod. 'Right now, I need you and your team to come through and get these young ones back. If someone's watching Bairstow, it's because Bairstow is a key to this. Emma Matthews, Bairstow. The kids will be somewhere around them.'

'I hope you're right,' said Hope. 'I'll be in my office until I get the shout. And then I'll be out there on it.'

'Take care,' said Macleod as Hope stood up. 'There are three wee ones in danger. Don't make it four.'

She was going to react. She was going to bite and tell him she could do her job and to back off. But he was right. Sometime soon, she'd have to step back. Not right now, though. Three other mothers needed her.

Chapter 22

Susan kept the car at a sensible distance behind Emma Matthews. She'd been driving now for the best part of two hours, and was just arriving at Inverness, turning off in towards the city. Emma then pulled up at a hotel close to a golf course. Susan stopped at the far end of the car park, and along with Perry, she watched Emma Matthews enter the hotel and not come out.

'So what do we do now?'

'Watch, I guess,' said Perry. 'I'll check with the boss.'

Perry placed a phone call to Hope.

'Where are you?' asked Hope.

'Hotel down the road from you. You can be here in about three minutes. She's gone in and hasn't come out. Haven't seen her go anywhere else. Looks like she's sitting tight.'

'Well, just keep watching,' said Hope. 'We're trying to monitor Bairstow's movements. We think that wherever he goes, the kids will not be that far away. They'll all be tied in to exposing Bairstow whenever they die. The idea being to put everything out in the press, including the deaths that happened on the road. That's the whole point of this, Perry.'

'True,' said Perry, 'but from a Matthews point of view, why is she up here? She must be going to make contact at some point. So I agree we sit tight.'

'Macleod has the same opinion. You sit and watch. He's involved Kirsten as well. I don't know exactly where she is, but she might be looking into Bairstow's movements.'

'We'll stay here,' said Perry. 'If somebody can pop down and relieve us for an hour, that would be good. We could do with a break.'

'We'll see what we can do,' said Hope. 'It could be a long one, though.'

The day passed without event, Emma Matthews remaining inside the hotel. Hope and Ross relieved Perry and Susan a few times. As it got into the late evening, the DI and DS drove out towards Lord Bairstow's estate, to keep an eye on him instead.

Around midnight, Emma Matthews stepped out of the hotel and back into her car. Susan was behind the wheel and began to tail her as Perry called up Hope.

'She's leaving,' he said to Hope.

'Stick with her. There's not much happening at this end. We're still over at Bairstow's. Came to watch his main residence right from when we left you. He spent the evening with friends, but they seem to be leaving now.'

Perry closed the call and sat back, peering for Emma Matthew's car up ahead. It was more difficult to tail at night in one sense, because you couldn't see the car ahead so clearly. All you saw was its red lights at the back and its beam at the front. If you lost track of it, confirming it was the same car was difficult.

Perry watched intently as Susan drove. They headed out of Inverness, eventually picking up another road. They weren't that far away from Lord Bairstow's estate, and would pass by it. Arriving in Contin, a small village, Emma Matthews passed out the other side, heading off towards Ullapool.

'She could, of course, still break out towards Kyle,' said Perry, 'but I don't see why. If the kids are going to be involved with Bairstow, they're going to have them close by, aren't they?'

'That makes sense,' said Susan. 'But where is she going to go?'

As they left Contin behind, the car ahead indicated and turned in to a car park.

'It's the Rogie Falls car park,' said Perry. 'Go past. Go down a bit, switch your lights off, turn round and come back.'

'Switch the lights off?' said Susan.

'Yes, we want to go past again or get up close, but she doesn't want to see it's us.'

Susan did as told and on the way back, drove past the Rogie Falls car park. Perry could see the car and could just about make out Emma Matthews getting out. As soon as they got past, Perry pointed for Susan, showing she should pull over at the side of the road. She found a lay-by not that far away and parked up.

Susan jumped out of the car. 'I'm going to keep an eye on where she is.'

'Don't go off on your own,' said Perry. 'Watch the car park. No further. If she disappears off towards the falls or anything, don't follow.'

Susan nodded while Perry called Hope.

'We've got people on the move here,' said Hope. 'I'm going to call Seoras.'

Perry received a call from Macleod two minutes later. 'I'm going to come out and join you,' he said. 'I'm bringing Kirsten with me. What's happening out there?'

'Susan's watching. I can't see from here, but Matthews was

in the car park. I've told Susan to go no further, just to watch the car park.'

'Good idea,' said Macleod. 'We'll wait until Kirsten's there. We'll be joining you shortly.'

A minute later, Susan got back into the car with Perry. 'She's got back in,' said Susan. 'I'll go back up and keep an eye, but I thought I should tell you.'

'Macleod's coming out,' said Perry. 'He's bringing Kirsten with him. He doesn't like this.'

'I don't like it either,' said Susan, 'but we still have those three kids to find.'

Susan headed back out while Perry sat waiting. It was twenty minutes later when there was a knock on the car door, causing Perry to jump. The rear door opened, and then the passenger one.

'Anything changed yet?' asked Macleod.

'No, she's still over there.'

'Susan?' said Kirsten. Perry nodded. 'I'll go get her.' Kirsten came back two minutes later. 'She's on the move.'

'You go ahead with Susan,' said Macleod. 'There's no point Perry and I trying to creep around. You two are better at that. We'll follow, though, at a distance, back you up.'

Kirsten gave him a look at the phrase 'back up,' but she simply nodded and disappeared off into the night.

Susan was lying down on a patch of grass close to the car park, watching as Emma Matthews disappeared into the dark of the path. There was a tap on her shoulder, and Kirsten whispered in her ear to get up. The night was dark making it hard to see your feet in front of you.

Emma Matthews shone a torch, but Kirsten wouldn't have any light. Together with Susan, she crept along the path a short distance behind Matthews.

Susan had been down to Rogie Falls before. It was a bright spot with a flowing river underneath the bridge. The path was enclosed by trees making it hard to see anything from, which meant that when you got to the bridge, the view was quite spectacular.

Walking along the path now, maintaining a distance and quiet, the place took on a completely different air. Susan could feel herself trembling, but she forced herself on and tried to take comfort because Kirsten was there.

Emma Matthews walked out onto the centre of the bridge and switched off her torch. Susan could see a flashlight on the other side; on and off, on and off. It could have been morse code for all she knew. And then somebody else approached the bridge.

'I'm going to get close,' said Kirsten. 'Stay here.'

Susan struggled to see Kirsten as she disappeared off into the dark, but she saw the man walking across the bridge with the torch. Matthews and he were speaking, but Susan wasn't close enough to hear. But she hoped Kirsten was.

Kirsten was currently just off the path in the undergrowth. She could see the man joining and thought about running across the bridge. The trouble was it was narrow—they would see her coming, for there was no shelter on the bridge. She heard the river gushing below. It was noisy for there had been rain the day before. She looked at the underside of the bridge and crept forward carefully and quietly. She snuck down until she was able to get under the bridge and crawled across underneath it, clinging to the metal framework that supported the wood of the structure . As she reached the centre she could overhear the conversation above.

'It's all done. It's all in place.'

'Are you sure?' said Emma.

'Did it ourselves.'

'Any risk though, that they'll wake?'

'No, we gave them the sleeping mixture, like you said. Be out like lights until the time comes, and if they don't wake up, well, it'll be all the better for them.'

'Good,' said Emma. 'We can all head home then, await developments. Get rid of the van. You don't need it anymore. Burn it out. Any news from the other side?'

'Last we knew, Bairstow was still entertaining his guests.'

'Well, entertainment's going to be his undoing, isn't it?' said Emma.

The man gave a laugh. 'Contact me in the usual way,' he said.

Kirsten heard the man walk away and then heard Emma Matthews striding off in the opposite direction. She hoped Susan would be able to cover and take out Emma Matthews, because the man was going to be important.

Underneath the bridge, Kirsten scrambled, climbing here and there as quietly as she could. By the time she got to the far side, the man was walking off the bridge and she could hear voices in the air. She clambered up through the undergrowth, out to where the path widened slightly. It would head up here towards the road, she was sure of it. It wasn't a public road, but it was one that would lead to one. As she peered out through the undergrowth, she saw the van up ahead.

'That's it, boys,' said the man. 'Time to go. Burn this sucker.'

Kirsten stepped out of the undergrowth, hurrying up behind the man. However, one of the other men switched on a torch, almost blinding her.

'What on earth?' said the torch bearer.

Kirsten saw a gun. She stepped forward, grabbing the man who had been on the bridge with an arm round his neck and throwing him hard to the ground. Her leg went up and kicked the gun from the other man's hand. She then approached a third, hitting him twice in the head with hard punches that made him tumble to the ground.

She turned back to the first man. He was now getting up to draw a gun. Kirsten was quicker though, scrambling forward, launching herself into the air, and caught him with a kick to the chin. He fell hard to the ground as she turned to the other men who were down, hitting them hard in the back. She reached inside her jacket and removed some plastic ties, tying the men's hands behind their backs. She then tied their feet together at the ankles, before she walked back over to the bridge.

'Are we done on that side?' she asked.

A torch was now on, and a woman was being marched across the bridge. As they got closer, the torch was twisted, and it sent a beam of light out everywhere. It was placed down on the ground, and Kirsten could see Susan's face. She was holding Emma Matthews tightly. Macleod and Perry emerged from behind the torch light.

'Is this everybody?' asked Macleod.

'They're alive. A couple of them are out cold,' said Kirsten, 'but they had guns as well. This is them. From what I heard, they've moved the babies. They said it's all set up, ready to go. They were all heading home.'

'What's it mean?' said Macleod to Emma. 'What's it all mean?'

'Oh no. Killed my father, didn't they? Killed my father. You'll get nothing from me. Bairstow will get plenty though. He'll get his comeuppance. You should have done better, Macleod.

You should have done more.'

'Do you want me to try to get something out of her?' said Kirsten.

'You can try,' said Macleod, 'but she won't talk. Not now. Not when she's so close.'

Perry went over to stand beside the men while Susan searched the van. But there was nothing. No details. No word to show where babies had been taken or held.

'Fresh out of ideas,' said Macleod, and he called Hope.

'Still sitting here watching. What's up at your end?' she asked.

'Our tail of Emma Matthews has ended. We've found the people with the van. We don't know where the babies are at the moment, but we know it's soon. It's imminent, because they've been put in place. You need to find them, Hope. It's going to be there, somewhere near Bairstow. Stop watching him. Go and ask him. Go and find out what's going on. The hand's been played now. We can't watch anymore.'

'Will do,' said Hope.

Macleod closed down the call. He turned and looked at Emma Matthews. 'Your father was a man of justice. He wanted to see everything out in the light. Look at you. You're becoming the thing that he stood up against.'

'My father was murdered, though, by the people you work for.'

'If you think that,' said Macleod, 'then there's not a lot more to be said between us.'

184

Chapter 23

'That was Seoras,' said Hope. 'He says we need to go to Bairstow. Emma Matthews has met up with three others, the ones that drove the van and dropped the bodies. She's not saying anything. But the van crew said that the wee ones are in place, whatever's happening to them. Seoras says it's tied in with Bairstow. He said stop watching him, just ask him, find out what's happening, and put a stop to it.'

Ross nodded and drove the car up to the front gates of the Bairstow estate. There was a hut from which a man emerged. He was dressed in a guard's uniform and wore a peaked cap. Slowly, he wandered over to the car, but Hope couldn't wait, opened the car door and came out towards him.

'Whoa, this is Lord Bairstow's estate. What do you want?'

Hope produced her warrant card from inside her jacket and held it up to him.

'DI Hope McGrath. I need to see Lord Bairstow straight away.'

'I'm not sure that's going to be possible.'

'What?' said Hope. 'You'll make it possible. And you'll make it possible now.'

'His Lordship didn't want to be disturbed. He's got guests at the moment, and this is an unholy hour to be coming, anyway. Can't you do it tomorrow?'

'Excuse me?' said Hope. 'You don't get to ask me that sort of question. You go back inside that hut, and you tell them I want to speak to him now. And you can open these gates so our car can get through.'

'I'm afraid I can't do that.'

'I'm afraid you'll have to work out how to do that,' said Hope. 'I am not sitting around here at His Lordship's beck and call. Get on that telephone and talk to him now.'

'Do you have any sort of warrant?'

'I'm not here to search the place,' said Hope. 'Although that could come shortly. I need to speak to His Lordship. Right now!'

The guard disappeared off but kept the gates locked. When he returned, he simply shook his head. ' His Lordship isn't receiving any more guests.' He turned and went back inside his hut.

'You can't be serious,' said Hope. 'You can't seriously tell me they want to go down this path.'

'Well,' said Ross, 'we've asked for access. They've said no. So, I guess we'll have to show that a crime is being committed. Have a suspicion to get ourselves in.'

'Back away for a minute,' said Hope. She turned and drove. Ross turned the car around, drove a little distance away, back to where they'd been watching it previously. As they sat there, Hope wondered the best way to approach this. She would need his cooperation, after all. Bairstow would know his grounds better than she would.

As she was pondering this, she felt her phone vibrate. She picked it up and put it to her ear. 'I don't want to tell you your job,' said a voice, 'but I would try the gates again.' Hope went to reply, but the line went dead.

'Who's that?' asked Ross.

'Somebody who told me to try the gates again. Move off, so we can see them.'

Ross turned the car and drove a little closer. He couldn't see the gates. Neither could Hope. He went closer still and then he realised the gates were there. But they were fully open. Ross drove the car just inside the gates and saw the hut where the security man would sit. He was lying on the ground.

Hope jumped out, went over to him. He had a pulse, and he was woozy, barely starting to come round. Hope jumped back in the car. 'Straight up to the house. Go.'

'Is he all right?'

'He's been knocked out.'

'Kirsten?' queried Ross.

'Kirsten was with Seoras. No, somebody else.'

As they arrived at the front door, a guard came running out of the house and Hope took out her warrant card as she strode over towards him. She put it up into his face. 'DI Hope McGrath. Lord Bairstow is in trouble.'

It was accurate, wasn't it? Or as accurate as it needed to be. Besides, it would get the guard's attention.

'What do you mean, he's in trouble?'

'Somebody's just broken onto your estate,' said Hope, pointing back down. 'Took out the security guard—'

'But he can't be disturbed.'

'Well, you better disturb him. He's under threat.'

The man looked at her, then at Ross, who nodded.

'Come with me,' he said. The man took them inside to a side room, just through the front door of the house. 'Wait here.

I'll go get him.' Another man entered and sat down on a seat, watching the pair of them.

'I just said his life's in danger, yet he can't be disturbed,' Hope whispered to Ross in the corner of the room. 'Why? What's he doing that his life being in danger isn't worth getting hold of him quicker?'

'Maybe he's with somebody he doesn't want to be seen with.'

'Well, we need to get out here, Ross.'

'Leave it to me.'

Ross walked across to the man stationed with them. 'I need the toilet, mate. Where do I go?' said Ross.

The man looked at him for a moment and then got up and opened the door, pointing across the hall. Ross turned, walked over, went through the open door, and then a second one, before closing that one behind him. The man left the first door open and waited until he saw Ross coming back.

'Your toilet's blocked,' said Ross. The man looked stunned. 'Your toilet, it's blocked. Come.'

Ross turned round, marching directly back to the toilet. The man got up and followed. Hope saw her opportunity. She followed them out of the door, quietly tiptoed across, and began climbing the stairs. She could see one of Bairstow's men up above walking along the landing, so she ducked in behind a large vase. From there, she carefully made her way up and saw two corridors. One ran down to lots of small doors. The other had only a few doors coming off of it. The carpet also looked a lot nicer. It was more industrial, more rough and ready in the smaller corridor.

Bairstow must be along the big one. That must be servants down to the right, she thought. She stood up tall and walked along the corridor, looking at the rooms on either side. The left-hand side had a guest bedroom, a second guest bedroom, and then a door that was unmarked. Clearly, it had a lot of room inside it, for the wall stretched further along the corridor. On the other side, a gym was noted, a living room, and a dining area. Hope went for the door that wasn't marked, but from the bedroom side. Approaching it, she knocked on it quickly.

'Come in,' said a voice. Hope pushed the door open, and then looked across to see Bairstow, standing in his underpants, trying to pull on some trousers.

'Getting changed,' said Hope.

'Get out,' said Bairstow.

'I don't think so,' said Hope. 'Where are you going?'

'What do you mean, where am I going? I've just entertained some guests. I'm not going anywhere.'

'Yet you've come in to change into, forgive me, what looks like a fresh pair of pants. And some trousers. Oh look, there's a shirt on the bed. Casual, but smart. Meeting someone?'

'It's none of your business what I'm doing. Get out, or I shall call your boss.'

'Call him. Call his boss. Call the one above that,' said Hope. 'I don't really care. I want to know where you're going.' She strode over to the window and pulled back the curtains. Looking down, she saw a car driving away.

'Who's in that car?'

'You have no business being here,' said Bairstow. 'No business at all. Get out.'

'We have three young babies whose deaths are going to be linked to you. I need to find them. You're the key. They are around you somewhere. I know this because the group who is going to kill them has told us. They told my boss that they will be killed and you will be in the spotlight. Therefore, it's

189

got to be here somewhere because this is where you are. So where are you going?'

Bairstow marched up to her and pushed a finger into the middle of Hope's chest. 'You need to leave now.'

He reached round with his hand to grab her arm and to escort her to the door. But Hope grabbed it and stuck it round behind his back. 'Don't assault a police officer,' she said. 'Just tell me where you are going.'

He hadn't quite pulled his trousers all the way up and fastened them. They descended back down again, leaving him in a comical position of having his arm pushed up behind his back and his trousers down round his ankles.

'You have no need for that knowledge.'

'I've told you why. I have every need. We're talking about three innocents.'

'Get your boss on the line, now!'

'I suggest you tell the detective inspector exactly where Lady Hereford is going.'

Hope looked round. There had only been the two of them in the room. Who was that? From out of the corner, a figure approached. It was smaller than Hope, older, with long black hair, but dressed all in black. Hope looked at Anna Hunt and saw Bairstow's cringe.

'What do you mean by this?' he said.

'Tell the detective inspector where Lady Hereford is going,' said Anna. 'It's in your best interests. It's in the best interests of the country. After all, that's who I serve, isn't it?'

Bairstow looked at her. 'Two-bit operator,' he said.

'The DI is, how shall we put it, bound not to break the law, bound not to abuse anyone she comes across. There to be helpful, there to be restrained. I'm not. Tell her where Lady

Hereford is going.'

'She's off to the pavilion.'

'Pavilion? Spot of cricket?' said Hope.

'No,' said Bairstow. 'Certainly not cricket.'

'Oh, it's not cricket, all right. Lord Hereford would certainly not enjoy this sort of match,' said Anna Hunt.

'What's the pavilion?' asked Hope.

'The pavilion is where Lord Bairstow likes to do his entertaining, of a more private nature.'

'You mean it's his—'

'Yes, it's his sordid little place where he takes the ladies to make sure that their husbands don't find out what they're up to with him,' said Anna.

'When's she off there?' said Hope, and then stopped for a moment. 'How does it work?' she said.

'What?' said Bairstow.

'How does it work?'

'What do you mean, how does it work? I'm a man, she's a woman.'

'No,' said Hope. 'What I mean is, how does this arrangement work?'

'I get in touch with her people. We plan it in advance, make sure he's not about.'

'No. How is it working tonight? Tell me the detail. Is there a timescale to be there?'

'She will be there at approximately 1:30. I'll be there by two.'

'Then that's what they're doing,' said Hope.

'Fill me in,' said Anna.

'The three babies who were kidnapped. They're here. We apprehended the people that did it. It's Emma Matthews who's involved,' said Hope.

'That's how she had all the information. All the people,' said Anna.

'From her father,' said Hope. 'Exactly. But Lady Hereford meets at half one. And then Bairstow is meant to follow at two. That means that whatever's going to happen will happen before two, but after half one.'

'What are you on about?' said Bairstow.

'You're going to be highlighted. You're going to be implicated in the hope that people will investigate you deeper. The way they're going to do that is they're going to kill Lady Hereford, along with several babies, on your property with you about to turn up.'

'That's preposterous. What have I got to do with any of it?'

'Don't,' said Hope. 'Lauren Starr is on your head. The fact we couldn't get to anyone else is on your head.' Hope turned to walk away, out of the room.

Suddenly, the door of the bedroom was thrown open again. A man was standing there with Ross.

'This guy, he's just pulled me about, sir. He's—'

'Let my sergeant go,' said Hope. 'Are you coming?' she said to Anna. 'We haven't got that long.'

Chapter 24

'Seoras, I've got where it's happening, or at least I think I do. It's a place called the Pavilion. It's on his estate, Bairstow's estate. You shouldn't be that far from it. Not if you were at Rogie.'

'I'm practically back in Inverness,' said Macleod. 'I've brought them in. Got Emma Matthews in the car, about to book her in. But Perry's still out there with Susan. They should be back soon. They were behind me. I headed off first. They were waiting for another couple of cars, but they should have picked up by now.'

'Let's hope so,' said Hope.

Hope dialled again, this time looking for Perry.

'Hello?' said Perry.

'A place called the Pavilion, Perry,' said Hope. 'You need to get there as soon as you can with Susan. Give me some backup.'

'We're just about to leave Rogie Falls.'

'Then you're not far away. Twenty minutes maybe. The Pavilion. Look it up. It's on the map.'

'Will do.' Hope closed down the call. 'Right, come on. Let's go, Ross,' she said. 'How long till we get there?'

'Thirty minutes. Maybe forty. We're not that close. He's clever where he's put the pavilion. It's at the far end of the estate. By the time we drive back onto roads and get round to it, we'll be double the time Perry will take.'

'Fast as you can,' said Hope. 'Fast as you can.'

* * *

'We've got to go,' said Perry to Susan. 'Get the wheel.'

Susan looked at him quite shocked, but ran to the front of the car and jumped in. She had the engine going, as Perry got in beside her, holding his phone in front of him.

'It's a place called The Pavilion on the estate.'

'Left or right out of the car park?' asked Susan.

'Stand by,' said Perry. Susan spun the car and drove up to the exit of the car park, waiting for Perry's instruction. As she halted, she heard the back door of the car open, and a woman with black hair jumped in.

'Kirsten,' said Susan.

'Where are you two off to in a hurry?'

'The Pavilion. Right,' said Perry. Susan put the foot down and drove off, almost sending Kirsten flying in the back seat.

'Why?' asked Kirsten.

'Hope said it. She reckons it's where the kids will be. She's on her way too, but I don't know, they might be behind us.'

Perry settled in, watching the road ahead. Susan flicked the lights on. This time she wasn't holding back, and Perry's hand reached up to the handle above his window.

'Go,' said Kirsten, 'go!'

As they got closer, Perry had to direct Susan, going left, then right, then down a small track, eventually pulling up in front of a pair of large, heavy gates.

'It's through there,' said Perry.

'Can you get them open?' asked Susan.

Perry stepped out of the car, running towards the gates, but Kirsten ran past him, jumped up, hurled herself over the gates, and began running on the other side.

Perry looked at the gates. There was a lock across them. He'd never get that open. He turned round to Susan. He waved at her, indicating that he couldn't open them. She got out of the car.

'Go,' she said, and she knelt down, putting her cupped hands out for Perry. He put a foot on her hands, and she pushed him up with every bit of ounce of strength she had. Perry just about reached the top of the gate, swung a leg up, and eventually fell down to the other side. As he got to his feet, Susan landed beside him.

'That building, that's the pavilion,' said Perry. The pavilion was small. A wooden lodge, but it had lights on the overhanging roof that lit up the patio at the front. Kirsten, however, was approaching slowly, almost as if she could see something.

Perry watched as she dropped, looking along at ground level. He crept up behind her with Susan and eventually stopped short of Kirsten. As he did so, the silence of the night was broken. He could hear a baby wailing.

'They're inside,' said Perry. 'They're inside. I'll go in and get them.'

'No, you won't,' said Kirsten. 'The moment you get inside this thing's going to blow.'

'What?' said Perry.

'It's got sensors in front there. You walk past there, there's a countdown to a bomb and I have no idea how long it's going to be.'

'A countdown to a bomb? Are you sure?'

Kirsten turned and looked at him. 'I have done this before.'

'So what? What was going to happen here then?' asked Susan.

'Well, he was coming here,' asked Kirsten. 'Why are you directed here?'

'I don't know.' Perry picked up his phone and called for Hope.

'Where are you, Perry?' asked Hope, answering the call.

'We're at the pavilion. Kirsten's with me. She says there's a bomb. There are sensors outside and she says if we approach, it'll set the sensor off and there's a bomb. She has no idea how long it'll take to blow up or what's going on. She wants to know why you've got us at the pavilion.'

'Bairstow was sending Lady Hereford here. Lady Hereford and he were going to have a night of it. Somebody knew that. Lady Hereford was going to be ahead by half an hour, forty minutes.'

'So, they were going to blow her up as well? Her and the babies. And Lady Hereford would be missing, having gone to Bairstow's. Lots of questions to ask. Lots of questions aimed at him.'

'So, what do we do?' said Perry.

'Ask Kirsten if she can defuse it.'

'Got Hope on the line,' said Perry to Kirsten. 'Can you defuse this? Can you get us in?'

'Not at the moment. I need to talk to some people.'

Perry watched as the woman started taking photographs. But she seemed to use something that wasn't producing normal photographs. There was a trace, a pattern, in front, possibly showing where sensors were.

'She doesn't know, Hope,' said Perry back on the phone.

'She's trying to get hold of someone who can help. She has no idea.'

'Lady Hereford will be arriving there in about five minutes. Any time between that and a half hour afterwards could be when they've set the bomb for her. I'd expect it wouldn't be that much longer.'

'There's definitely babies in there. I can hear them,' said Perry.

'I'm getting there as quick as I can,' said Hope. 'This is your call, Perry. Look to Kirsten's lead, but it's your call.'

'That's understood,' said Perry, and closed down the call.

'What's up?' asked Susan.

'In five minutes' time, Lady Hereford will be here. That place, that's where Bairstow and her were going to have a night of it. I think the aim was to blow her up in there with the babies. Pull Bairstow in. Make it a public spectacle. Lots of questions for him to answer.'

'You're telling me that this thing could be, what, set to go off?' asked Susan.

'I don't know. Well, they may have set a sensor on it, so if anybody went in, it would then blow after a period of time. But they could also have a separate switch on it. That makes it go off whenever. If Lady Hereford binned the idea for any reason, you'd still have an explosion in his estate with babies in it,' said Kirsten. 'I need to talk to someone.'

Perry stood, feeling a little helpless. His eyes fixed on Kirsten as she spoke to someone. Kirsten turned round to Perry, her hand over the phone. 'I'm speaking to Anna Hunt. Anna's in the area, but Anna cannot get here for at least another twenty minutes, fifteen tops. Anna has something that could clear this up. We need to be able to wait fifteen or twenty minutes.'

Perry shook his head. 'It's not what Hope said. We need to go in now.'

'Perry,' said Kirsten. 'If we go in now, we could walk into that building and the whole lot could explode in our faces. As quick as that.'

'Are you sure, though?' asked Perry. 'Wouldn't they put a delay on it? Wouldn't there be some sort of—'

'There could be,' said Kirsten. 'But until I can assess where the device is to be able to switch it off, I can't tell you what that time rate is. The type of device—we'll need to locate that and find it. Anna Hunt has in her car what we need. She's on her way. She'll be fifteen minutes.'

Perry called Hope back. He could feel the sweat pouring down his head now.

'Hope. Kirsten says she can't do anything here. She needs Anna Hunt. Anna Hunt's got equipment that could defuse this. She could find it and then switch it off. Just confirm to me,' said Perry, 'Lady Hereford was going to be here when?'

'You're into the time when she would have arrived.'

'And then, when was Bairstow going to come?'

'After her, he said. It could be half an hour, but it could be 15 minutes. Perry, we're on borrowed time here. There's no saying what's going to happen now.'

'Are you telling me that this house could go up? This place could just blow with those kids inside?' said Perry.

'If that's what Kirsten says, that she can't diffuse it, yes. Your only option is to wait. I'm telling you to wait. Perry, I'm telling you to wait, okay?'

'There are kids inside, Hope. Babies. Three of them.'

'Perry, trust me. I'm feeling that more than anyone. But you can't go in. You cannot risk yourself. The three of you stay out. Let Anna get there. Then we'll deal with it.'

Perry closed down the call. He looked at Kirsten. 'If you were setting this bomb, how long would you wait? How long from Lady Hereford arriving?'

'I don't know,' said Kirsten. 'They're going to be pretty tight on the timescale, aren't they? If they've got a time for it, Bairstow must have made plans. Hereford's arrival. Maybe she was meant to be disappearing somewhere else, pretending to stay the night there. This is going to be a tight window.'

'Honestly,' said Perry, looking at Kirsten. 'Tell me, if we wait fifteen minutes, do you think that place will go up?'

Kirsten thought for a moment. 'I'm sorry,' she said. 'Yes. Yes, but we have to wait. We go in, we all die.'

'How long a time would we get?'

'There's no way of knowing,' said Kirsten. 'It could be immediate.'

'If you were setting it,' said Perry, 'how long would you give?'

'I'd make sure they were inside. I'd make sure there were no survivors. Allow whatever staff is with her to go in, too. Somebody to take bags from the car. Maybe she's getting dressed. Two minutes. I'd probably allow two minutes, tops.'

'So, we'd have two minutes.'

'I didn't say that,' said Kirsten. 'I said that's what I would do. This thing could go up as soon as you go in.'

'Perry,' said Susan, 'you can't. You can't.'

On the air, Perry could hear the cry. There were two babies crying now, both wailing. 'I'm not giving them up,' said Perry. Before anyone could stop him, he sprinted forward.

'Get him back,' said Susan to Kirsten. But Kirsten was already on her feet.

'He's tripped it anyway,' she cried, and tore off after Perry.

Perry hit the pavilion veranda, leaping up onto it, arriving at the door and pushing at it. It opened easily, already unlocked. *Well, that was something*, thought Perry.

He stepped inside, into a wooden hallway. There was a cry from the left-hand side. He tore off over that way. Pushing open the door, he saw a cot. There were two babies inside. One was lying sleeping. The other one was wailing.

He heard Kirsten come in the door behind him. 'Here,' he said. He reached down and grabbed one baby and threw the child across the room. Kirsten grabbed one. Then Perry threw the second one.

'There's a third.'

Kirsten scanned the room. 'Corner. Over there in the corner. Cardboard box.'

There was crying coming from the box, and Perry ran over. Susan appeared at the door and Kirsten yelled at her to get out. Perry picked up the baby and turned. There was no longer a Kirsten at the door—she had fled, baby in either hand. Perry got to the door, turned through the hallway and saw the front door lying open, Kirsten clearing the patio, Susan running out in front.

As Perry got through the hall and out onto the patio, he saw Susan turning, looking back for him. There was a loud bang. The world changed; heat roared from behind him. The start of a cry of his name came from Susan's lips. Perry leapt from the patio for all he was worth.

His arms were wrapped around the child, and the force of an explosion drove him. He turned over and landed with his back hitting the ground. He rolled three times, desperately clinging to the child. His head banged off something as he stopped rolling on his back. His arms collapsed off the child.

A pain shot through his shoulder, all around his back, and Perry screamed out loud. He could see fires around him. There was still heat coming from the building.

'Perry!' screamed Susan. 'Perry!'

Then he saw Kirsten Stewart's face. It was all he could see. A hand was slapping his cheek. 'Can you hear me, Perry? Perry, can you hear me?' And the darkness set in.

Chapter 25

'How many times have you walked along these corridors?'

Macleod turned round and looked at the Assistant Chief Constable. 'It's not a question I get asked very often,' he told Jim. 'I don't know. Thankfully, I haven't had to visit anyone who's died yet.'

'So you'd dread that day. Do you expect it?' asked Jim.

'I don't know. I try not to think about it. Perry lost a lot of blood, though, from the head wound, lacerations across the back.'

'It's been three days, though. At least he should be sitting upright.'

Macleod entered the lift and rode up along with Jim until they got off on the fourth floor and walked over to a ward. There was a policeman standing outside a private room, and as Macleod approached, he stood up.

'Sir, sir,' said the constable.

'It's all right,' said Macleod.

'Angus, isn't it?' said Jim.

'Yes, it is, Assistant Chief Constable.'

'Jim,' he said. 'How's our patient inside?'

'I believe the doctor's with him at the moment.'

'In that case, we'll wait,' said Jim.

The three men stood outside the room, and the constable was clearly agitated. Macleod thought it must have been a nice number, just sitting guarding a room that, well, really, nobody was going to go into unless they were from the force. Macleod thought it advisable, though. He wasn't sure about retaliations. Maybe there would be. Maybe there wouldn't. There'd been an explosion on Bairstow's estate, so it was in the news.

The kids were safe, returned now, and that was a sigh of relief for everyone. But Perry had not been so lucky.

The doctor came out, and Macleod stopped him. 'We just want to go in and see him. Is that okay? Can I ask how he is?'

'He's recovering,' said the doctor. 'He'll be another week, at least. We want to make sure he's okay and that shoulder sets properly. We popped it back in, but there was a lot of damage around it, too. He'll be okay.'

'That's good to know,' said Macleod. 'Thank you for your work.'

'He saved three kids,' said the doctor. 'Incredibly brave.'

'Yes,' said Macleod. 'Incredibly.' He entered the private room, followed by Jim, and left the constable outside.

Perry was sitting upright in bed, but with his eyes closed. As they got closer, they flicked open.

'Ah,' said Perry, 'Detective Chief Inspector, Assistant Chief Constable.'

Jim stepped forward and went to shake Perry's hand, but Perry offered him the left hand instead. 'If you're going to shake something, shake that one,' said Perry. 'I don't want to move the other one.'

'Of course not,' said Jim. 'Bloody well done. Bloody well done. You're a damn hero.'

'Three of them got out,' said Perry. 'All three of them.'

'I had word from Kirsten,' said Macleod. 'She said you were very brave, but you were also very stupid.'

'Couldn't take a risk on the kids. Couldn't take a risk by waiting. With all due respect, that's not what I do. They needed help. I couldn't guarantee they'd be okay unless I got them.'

'For what it's worth, they found the device,' said Macleod. 'Apparently, they've been able to do some work on it. If you hadn't have gone in, they'd have been dead.'

'Well, thank you, sir,' said Perry. 'What's the state of play, though? I've been kind of out of it for three days.'

'Well, it's not been easy going,' said Macleod.

'Can't we get Bairstow for any of this?'

'For what?' said Macleod. 'For what? We can't prove anything regarding the murder of Lauren Starr. We have got no evidence on him. Everything's supposition. If we're going to go after a fish like him, it needs to be watertight.'

'And even then,' said Jim, 'I don't know if you can even make it stick.'

'What about the rest of them?' said Perry. 'You got some people, didn't you? We got Emma Matthews.'

'We did get Emma Matthews. But she is not saying a word. Neither are the men from the van. We can tie the van to them. We can probably charge them eventually with the murder of our three unfortunates. They were dumped on the road. We'll be able to link it through, eventually. But they're not talking about the wider group. That's the problem, Perry. This isn't a case where we just charge people. There's more going on here.'

'So, what do you do about that?' asked Perry.

'I don't know yet. I really don't know.'

There was a knock on the door and Hope arrived, stepping inside with Susan Cunningham. Susan had an enormous bunch of flowers. She made her way over.

'Excuse,' said Perry, smiling. 'Let the lady through.'

Macleod stepped back, as did Jim. Susan approached the bed.

'You good?' she asked.

'Yes. How are you?' said Perry.

'I'm fine. I had a couple of bruises, that was it. Not like you. Scared me,' she said. 'You really scared me.'

From behind her, Hope looked over. 'You didn't follow orders,' said Hope.

'Would you?' asked Perry.

'No,' said Hope. 'I'm glad you got them.'

'Not as glad as I was. Kirsten was great,' he said. 'I couldn't have got out with all three of them. She didn't hesitate. As soon as I'd broke the line, as soon as I'd activated the device, she came straight in with me. So did Susan.'

'That's my team,' said Macleod. 'Expect nothing less from you.'

'Well done. Well done, indeed,' said Jim.

Susan looked round for a moment, and then said, 'Excuse me.' She leaned forward, put her arms around Perry, squeezing him tight and causing him to wince. But he didn't complain. She planted a kiss on the side of his cheek.

'Thank God you're alive,' she said. 'You scared me, you damn well scared me.'

'This is me,' said Perry.

'Our Perry running into the fray,' said Hope. 'Maybe we should give—'

The door opened again behind them, and Susan let go of

Perry. Another enormous bunch of flowers was entering the room, but this time Tanya was behind them. It was clear she'd clocked Susan hugging Perry. She walked over, put the flowers on the end of the bed, ignored everyone else, and walked straight up to Perry.

'I'm glad you're alive.' She bent down and kissed him on the opposite cheek from Susan.

'I can see this is more of a team moment,' said Jim. 'I'll step outside.'

'I'll join you,' said Macleod. He turned and on the way past for the door, he whispered in Hope's ear. 'Just make sure the two of them don't rip him to shreds fighting over him,' he said.

Hope smiled. 'I got them, Seoras.'

'You did well,' Macleod said. 'You did really well. But it's not over.'

Hope nodded, and Macleod followed Jim out of the door. As they stood outside, Ross came from the other direction.

'Just been parking the car, sir,' he said to Macleod.

'Good, Ross. Go on in. The whole team's in there, including Tanya.'

'Susan in too?' said Ross. Macleod nodded, raising his eyes.

'Better get in then. Save the poor man.' Ross entered the room.

Jim turned to Macleod. 'He called you "sir." You normally turn around and tell everyone else it's not "sir."'

'He always calls me "sir," does Ross. Can't get him not to. Leans too heavy on me that one. Trying to wean him off, but not easy, but he's good, he's clever. Hope needs him.'

'It's been awkward,' said Jim. 'Been very awkward, been getting a lot of heat from above. With what happened before with Hope, and that case where she stopped the bomb flooding that village, when I was in the wrong, it's been hard to reach back into your team.'

'Water under the bridge, Jim,' said Macleod. 'Water under the bridge. I told them. I said, "Jim, you may not like what he does, how he goes about it, or any of that, but he's a good cop, a good man, and he's trustworthy."'

'Thank you,' said Jim. 'We need to work out what's happening next. You're getting yanked this way and that, Seoras—both of us. Yanked by one lot, and the other lot, taking potshots at your team. This has to stop, and it won't stop now. Bairstow is in the news, but that's it. We haven't convicted anybody of anything. We have stopped nothing.'

'Had some minor victories. Isabella Isbister for one.'

'Is currently leading a secret life thanks to Anna Hunt,' said Jim. 'She's alive, and she's free from the man she was with. Yes, that's a victory, but it's not conclusive. The war is going on. The war. Because that's what this is. This is a war that's happening between two sides and we are stuck in the middle. And the public is going to get more and more affected.'

'What are you saying?' asked Macleod.

'I'm saying—well, let me take you to lunch.'

'Lunch?'

'Lunch,' said Jim. 'There's a nice restaurant I know, it's very quiet though, not many people go there, village outside of Inverness.'

'They do lunch, do they?'

'No, they don't, but I know the owner. They'll do lunch for me. You and I don't want to be seen doing this, so we won't. We need to plan, and we need to work out the next steps. We go on the offensive.'

'Good to know, sir,' said Macleod.

'Do you want to go back in and say goodbye to Perry before we leave?' said Jim.

'He'll be back in soon enough,' said Macleod. 'Besides, Perry's troubles are only just beginning. I don't want to be in there at the moment. I can't think of anything more damaging to a man than two women after him. One's a delight. Two is hell on earth. Especially for a man like Perry. He won't want to let either of them down.'

'You'll have to steer him through it,' said Jim.

'I've had questions from both of them. Asking about Perry. What's he like? I don't give out advice like that. For the best part of twenty years of my life, I was a constipated fool with regard to women. And that after starting off with one of the best. No, he's on his own with that one. Where do you say this restaurant was anyway?'

Epilogue

S eoras Macleod sat behind his desk. Behind him, the night was dark, although the streetlights were still on. This close in to the city, they never went off, and Macleod sometimes wished they did. He was happy enough sitting through the small hours, but he preferred it to be darker outside while he kept a low lamp on. He got up and closed the blinds, and the room went completely dark. His computer was off, so he reached over and flicked on his desk lamp.

There was a quiet knock on the door, and Macleod gave a gruff 'Come in.' The door opened, and he saw the red hair, and the long blue jeans of a six-foot detective inspector.

'I get worried about you sometimes,' said Hope. 'If I didn't know better, I would have thought you called me into your office at a late hour for something untoward.'

'You got a problem with being here?' asked Macleod.

'Tanya's from an HR background; you know that, don't you? I thought she would have advised you by now that you don't invite the younger woman into your office at a late hour, and then have all the lights off.'

'Coffee's on the desk there,' he said. Hope nodded and poured herself a cup and noted Macleod's steaming cup already on the desk.

She sat down in one of the seats opposite. There were three seats there.

'Am I getting a taste of déjà vu here?'

'There might be a few others to come,' said Macleod. 'How are you anyway, before they arrive?'

'I'm okay. But going forward, I'm not sure I can keep going. I may need to take more of a backward role, more of an advisory one.'

'Why don't you take maternity? Why don't you just go on the sick, then take your maternity, have your baby?'

'I'm not leaving you at the moment,' said Hope. 'If all I can do is advise, if all I can do is help you put the chess pieces out there, then that's what I'll do. And I'll stay in the office.'

'Okay,' said Macleod, 'but you do not risk that little one for anything.'

'When Perry said about the bomb being triggered and having to go for the babies, I wondered if I would have gone for them. Do you know that? I normally would have gone for them. I'm not sure I would have done this time, though. This one in here would have kept me from doing it.'

'Perry wouldn't have let you do it, anyway. Pregnant woman. Perry would just charge in ahead of you.'

'Well,' said Hope. 'Maybe I need to change the plan at the moment. But you've still got this brain.'

'That's good to know,' said Macleod.

There was another knock at the door. Only this time, the person didn't wait. The knock was loud, thunderous almost. And the door flew open. It was accompanied by a 'Bloody hell, Seoras!' The door slammed behind.

'Frank and I were out tonight. Do you know that? You've upset my plans. We were out to the theatre and then we were going to—'

'I don't need to know any more detail,' said Macleod.

'Well, actually, you do. It was my big night. Frank was in an amorous mood. Do you know what Frank likes to do?'

'Don't,' said Macleod.

'I had the outfit all ready,' said Clarissa.

'Would you shut her up?' Macleod said to Hope. He was laughing. 'I do not need to hear about the sexual exploits of Frank and Clarissa.'

'Don't pull me out here at this time of night, on the night when I'm getting what a good girl deserves.'

'How can you not use any graphic words and yet paint me the worst picture going?' said Macleod.

Clarissa stepped forward, swung her hand out, barely missing his head. 'It's a beautiful image,' she said. 'You remember that.' She sat down with a swish of her shawl and then stood up again to pour herself coffee. 'And you could have poured one for me instead of sitting there like my lord.'

'Can I just point out that, once again, I am the Detective Chief Inspector. The "chief" bit is very, very important. It distinguishes me from the other inspectors in the room.'

'Lack of manners is what distinguishes you,' said Clarissa, sitting down.

There was a quiet rap on the door. 'Come in,' said Macleod.

The door opened and a man dressed in combat fatigues and a hoodie stepped inside. Macleod wasn't sure what the creature was on the hoodie, but the word 'con' was there somewhere. Apparently, it meant 'convention.' Macleod was learning slowly about Emmett. But it was slow.

'Good evening,' said Emmett. 'Hope. Clarissa. I assume this is an important meeting.' He sat down quietly, then stood up. 'A coffee for everyone,' he said, despite the fact they were already three cups out and being drunk.

'Of course,' said Macleod, standing up and pouring a cup for Emmett. 'Here you go, Detective Inspector. Grab a pew.'

'Bloody cheek,' said Clarissa. 'You didn't pour me one.'

'He didn't take a swipe at my head.'

'Anyway,' said Hope. 'That's the three of us. That's three seats. What are we talking about?'

'Just a moment,' said Macleod. He picked up his phone. 'They're here,' he said briefly into it, and put the phone down.

Hope looked at him. 'We getting outfits or something? You doing a team photo?'

'Someone wants to speak to you,' said Macleod.

There was a rap at the door. Macleod told them to come in. Three detective inspectors turned and saw the Assistant Chief Constable make his way into the room. He came and stood beside Macleod's desk. Hope went to stand, but Jim put his hand out.

'No, no, no. Sit down, the three of you. I'll take up just a few minutes of your time,' said Jim. 'Earlier today, I went with your boss to have a discussion about recent events. I'm not happy, to say the least. You all know that there's a group who follow Forseti out there, trying to make their own law. There's another group that Emma Matthews seems to be a part of, trying to take Forseti's group out. We nearly lost three infant lives because of it. We've lost a retired service agent because of it.

'You have been shot at,' he said, pointing to Emmett. 'You had to climb aboard a boat and bring back a knife. A boat that was then exploded and you just about got away with it,' Jim said to Hope. 'In your current state, for want of a better word, it's not acceptable. And Clarissa had to go to the far reaches of Europe to learn about this group. And I'm rightly instructed that if it wasn't for a certain former Service agent and friend of your boss, it might have ended badly a few times as well. You've all been put through the mill in trying to defend the public and bring some justice. I want you to understand, this is a war,' said Jim, quite seriously. 'And we have only engaged in the first battles.

'We didn't choose it, but it's there. As of tonight, I have given Detective Chief Inspector Macleod instruction that he has the right to use any of you and your teams as he sees fit. He has been instructed to find this group and bring it to justice. That's the Forseti group. He has been instructed to find the other group and bring them to justice. I will pool as many resources as possible to that but this will be done quietly. This will be done with reports to me and to me only. Do I trust our Chief Constable? Yes, I do, but while we have a good person in charge, I don't wish to compromise that. In case this all goes south, there needs to be somebody with backbone maintaining the ship and able to step in if our efforts fail.

This won't be easy and it's up to you if you choose to come in on it. In your current state, again apologies for the word,' said Jim turning to Hope, 'if you want to take extended leave and go have your child before coming back, you're more than welcome to excuse this one. I can't ask you to put your child's life at risk.'

'So there it is,' said Macleod. 'Jim said that I should ask you all if you were okay to be part of this. I said you would be. You didn't need asked. But he said he wanted to hear it from you all.'

'Understand this,' said Jim, and his fist tightened. 'These

213

bastards were going to kill children, to make a point. They come after us? Fine. We're police officers. I expect flak. I expect things to come. They go after the public? Not fine. But they go after kids? They steal babies and are prepared to just blow them up? No. We get these bastards. And we get those who are slandering our own name, making justice that isn't. You may not think much of me as an officer, but I know what's right and what's wrong. And we need to step on this. So what do you say?'

Emmett stood up first and put his hand out. 'Gladly,' said Emmett. 'Gladly.'

Hope stood up too. 'Well, you're going to need a level head. So I'm in.'

Clarissa was sitting down. 'Bastards,' she said. 'You're damn right, Jim. Bastards. Let's get them.'

'Thank you all,' said Jim. 'I'll see you tomorrow, Seoras.' Jim turned to the door and walked out, closing it behind him.

'Right then,' said Clarissa, 'what do we do?'

'Well, I have a thought,' said Emmett. 'I was thinking that if we go back over and into—'

Macleod put his hand up. 'Whoa. Tomorrow. Okay? Tomorrow morning, 9a.m. The whole team. Every single one of them.'

'Pats will be on board,' said Clarissa. 'I can't ask the other two—'

'Yes, you can,' said Macleod.

'I don't know if they'll—'

'Then you can ask them. You've picked them; they'll do it. I have no doubt of that. Okay, everyone?'

'Will Perry be in tomorrow?' said Hope.

'Perry will be on board, but Perry will still be in hospital.

214

You can take him through it when you visit him,' said Macleod. '9 a.m. tomorrow morning. I'll see the three of you then and thank you.'

Emmett stepped forward and shook Macleod's hand. 'Always,' he said.

Clarissa pointed at him. 'You get me into some nonsense, don't you?' She gave him a grin. 'I'm off home for my sex.'

Macleod grinned back. 'Too much,' he said.

Hope hung back for a moment and when the other two had left the room, she said, 'You sure about this?'

'You're asking me if I'm sure?'

'I know you're sure. Understand, I'll be right behind you. I might not be able to run with you. It might be more of a waddle.'

'I welcome every bit of advice you can give me. But you keep that one safe.'

Hope nodded. She went to walk away, but then she walked round the desk, and she hugged Macleod. 'You don't do this lightly. I hope we make it out the other side.'

'We will,' he said. 'We will. Go home. Get a night of rest with John.'

Hope disappeared out of the office, and Macleod turned and opened up the blinds again. He switched off the desk lamp and stood looking out from the dark office. As he did so, he thought he could feel something, a presence, and then something touched his shoulder. He jumped and then caught himself.

'He makes quite the speech, your Assistant Chief Constable, doesn't he?'

'Have you been here the whole time, Anna?' said Macleod.

'I was coming to see you. I wanted a chat. You see, I thought

I might pop in and say well done to Perry. Although he'll never join the Service. You have to be able to wait things like that out.'

'He got the kids,' said Macleod. 'That's what he cared about.'

'Yes. Yes, he did. It's not what you cared about. Ultimately, you care about the overall picture. Jim's speech to them rallied the troops, but he's given it to you to spearhead.'

'What's wrong?' said Macleod. 'You think this is the wrong way to do it? You think it should be handed over to yourselves in the Service?'

'No,' said Anna. Macleod felt his hand being grabbed by hers, and she squeezed it tightly. 'I'm right here. You've got me on board. I will help you in any way I can to bring down both of these groups. Feel free to call me, and ask for help at any time. Feel free to ask for protection at any time. And keep Kirsten very close.'

'She was close last time. Our foul-mouthed friend doesn't always listen.'

'Keep her close,' said Anna. And she squeezed Macleod's hand. 'And it's a good job your Jane's a good woman,' said Anna.

'What do you mean by that?' said Macleod. He felt Anna's hand slip away from him, and she turned, walking over to the office door. She opened it and stepped outside. But before she could close it, Macleod said again, 'What do you mean by that?'

'If she wasn't nice, if she wasn't someone worthy of you, I might be tempted myself.'

'Too much going on to be thinking like that,' said Macleod.

'You're probably right,' said Anna. Macleod heard the door click closed. He turned and looked at it. The room was dark.

He could barely see. But he had to admit to himself that if Jane wasn't there, and despite what Anna Hunt was and what she did, she did leave an impression on him. One that he couldn't quite get away from. He turned back to look out the window. Tomorrow was a new day. It was a new battle. But right now, it was the same old war.

Read on to discover the Patrick
Smythe series!

READ ON TO DISCOVER THE PATRICK SMYTHE SERIES!

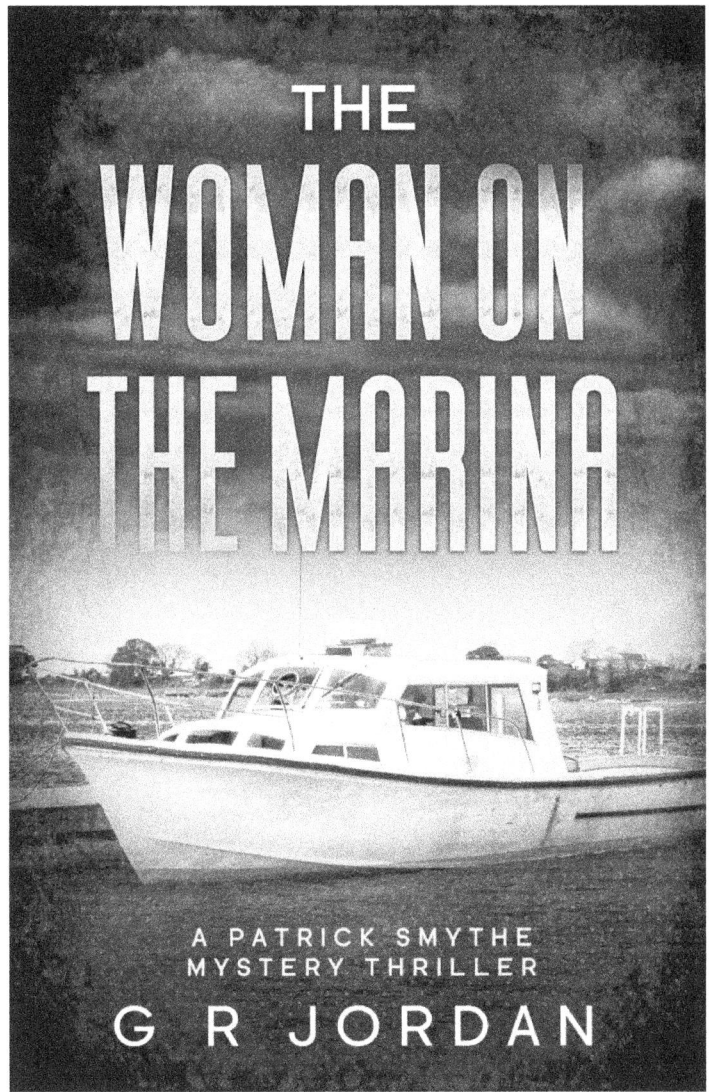

THE

WOMAN ON

THE MARINA

A PATRICK SMYTHE
MYSTERY THRILLER

G R JORDAN

Patrick Smythe is a former Northern Irish policeman who after suffering an amputation after a bomb blast, takes to the sea between the west coast of Scotland and his homeland to ply his trade as a private investigator. Join Paddy as he tries to work to his own ethics while knowing how to bend the rules he once enforced. Working from his beloved motorboat 'Craigantlet', Paddy decides to rescue a drug mule in this short story from the pen of G R Jordan.

Join G R Jordan's monthly newsletter about forthcoming releases and special writings for his tribe of avid readers and then receive your free Patrick Smythe short story.

Go to https://bit.ly/PatrickSmythe for your Patrick Smythe journey to start

About the Author

GR Jordan is a self-published author who finally decided at forty that in order to have an enjoyable lifestyle, his creative beast within would have to be unleashed. His books mirror that conflict in life where acts of decency contend with self-promotion, goodness stares in horror at evil, and kindness blindsides us when we at our worst. Corrupting our world with his parade of wondrous and horrific characters, he highlights everyday tensions with fresh eyes whilst taking his methodical, intelligent mainstays on a roller-coaster ride of dilemmas, all the while suffering the banter of their provocative sidekicks.

A graduate of Loughborough University where he masqueraded as a chemical engineer but ultimately played American football, Gary had worked at changing the shape of cereal flakes and pulled a pallet truck for a living. Watching vegetables freeze at -40'C was another career highlight and he was also one of the Scottish Highlands "blind" air traffic controllers.

These days he has graduated to answering a telephone to people in trouble before telephoning other people to sort it out.

Having flirted with most places in the UK, he is now based in the Isle of Lewis in Scotland where his free time is spent between raising a young family with his wife, writing, figuring out how to work a loom and caring for a small flock of chickens. Luckily, his writing is influenced by his varied work and life experience as the chickens have not been the poetical inspiration he had hoped for!

You can connect with me on:
- https://grjordan.com
- https://facebook.com/carpetlessleprechaun

Subscribe to my newsletter:
- https://bit.ly/PatrickSmythe

Also by G R Jordan

G R Jordan writes across multiple genres including crime, dark and action adventure fantasy, feel good fantasy, mystery thriller and horror fantasy. Below is a selection of his work. Whilst all books are available across online stores, signed copies are available at his personal shop.

 **Save The King (Highlands & Islands Detective Book 45**
https://grjordan.com/product/save-the-king
Macleod on the hunt for the Forseti group. A mole passing information to a group of killers. Can Macleod manage two evils or will pandemonium reign in this bloodiest of feuds?

DCI Seoras Macleod, tasked with finding the elusive Forseti group, sets his team to find their chain of command and high ruler. But with every discovery, they are plagued by suspects dying before they can be arrested. With his team working on two fronts, Macleod is stretched in both directions and finds it difficult to trust the very force he has worked with all his life. As he closes in on the higher echelons of the Forseti group, Macleod must tread the thin line between trust and betrayal to shut down both sets of killers to save his most prized arrest.

When there's no innocents around, who should the law protect?

Kirsten Stewart Thrillers
https://grjordan.com/product/a-shot-at-democracy
Join Kirsten Stewart on a shadowy ride through the underbelly of the Highlands of Scotland where among the beauty and splendour of the majestic landscape lies corruption and intrigue to match any city. From murders to extortion, missing children to criminals operating above the law, the Highland former detective must learn a tougher edge to her work as she puts her own life on the line to protect those who cannot defend themselves.

Having left her beloved murder investigation team far behind, Kirsten has to battle personal tragedy and loss while adapting to a whole new way of executing her duties where your mistakes are your own. As Kirsten comes to terms with working with the new team, she often operates as the groups solo field agent, placing herself in danger and trouble to rescue those caught on the dark side of life. With action packed scenes and tense scenarios of murder and greed, the Kirsten Stewart thrillers will have you turning page after page to see your favourite Scottish lass home!

There's life after Macleod, but a whole new world of death!

Jac's Revenge (A Jac Moonshine Thriller #1)

https://grjordan.com/product/jacs-revenge

An unexpected hit makes Debbie a widow. The attention of her man's killer spawns a brutal yet classy alter ego. But how far can you play the game before it takes over your life?

All her life, Debbie Parlor lived in her man's shadow, knowing his work was never truly honest. She turned her head from news stories and rumours. But when he was disposed of for his smile to placate a rival crime lord, Jac Moonshine was born. And when Debbie is paid compensation for her loss like her car was written off, Jac decides that enough is enough.

Get on board with this tongue-in-cheek revenge thriller that will make you question how far you would go to avenge a loved one, and how much you would enjoy it!

 **A Giant Killing (Siobhan Duffy Mysteries #1)**
https://grjordan.com/product/a-giant-killing
A body lies on the Giant's boot. Discord, as the master of secrets has been found. Can former spy Siobhan Duffy find the killer before they execute her former colleagues?

When retired operative Siobhan Duffy sees the killing of her former master in the paper, her unease sends her down a path of discovery and fear. Aided by her young housekeeper and scruff of a gardener, Siobhan begins a quest to discover the reason for her spy boss' death and unravels a can of worms today's masters would rather keep closed. But in a world of secrets, the difference between revenge and simple, if brutal, housekeeping becomes the hardest truth to know.

The past is a child who never leaves home!